Editing: Lori White Creative Editing Services

Cover Design: Dar Albert, Wicked Smart Designs

Proofreader: Melinda Kaye Brandt

 Created with Vellum

THE SCOUNDREL

A STEAMY ROMANTIC SUSPENSE

CLUB SOUTHSIDE

DELTA JAMES

Dedicated to My Two Best Friends:
Renee and Chris, without whom none of
what I do would be possible and to the Girls,
who bring joy to my life every single day

PROLOGUE

Chicago had a new lifestyle club that put the others to shame. The famous—or infamous, depending upon your point of view—Baker Street in London had branched out to Chicago. Like Baker Street for the U.K., Club Southside was the American headquarters for the covert operations group known around the world as Cerberus.

CHAPTER 1

KING

Undisclosed Location
Two Years Ago

Kingston Coltraine lay on his cot, staring up into nothingness. He'd lost count of the days he'd been here. Accused of acts of high treason and murder, his questioning had been unorthodox, to say the least. He hadn't been arrested; he'd been renditioned.

"Rendition," he snorted.

'Rendition' was the practice of covertly transporting suspected terrorists, criminals, or those a government feared could reveal truths it would rather never saw the light of day to be interrogated in a country whose human rights policies were virtually non-existent and generally never included such niceties as the humane treatment of prisoners.

The *drip, drip, drip* from the corner of his cell was relentless. Thoughts… the kind that did no one any good, ever, assailed him continuously. As he had no window, King had begun to wonder if the cell he was being held in was underwater. If it was beneath the surface, was it watertight or was the unrelenting falling water just a precursor for being drowned? The memory of a film he'd seen of a scuttled submarine's crew during the Civil War came unbidden and he pushed the grisly thought away.

He would not allow himself the luxury of believing his torture would be over soon and end in death. No, instead, he refused to give up hope that somehow he would find his way out to the other side and live free once again. Those who thought to end him would find he was one tough motherfucker to kill.

Footsteps from outside the door alerted King that they were coming again. He tried to take a deep breath, the effort reminding him that most likely his ribs were broken and one of his lungs had collapsed. It hurt like a sonofabitch to breathe.

Those who had tortured him had been well trained. They burned and cauterized wounds, beat and blistered his feet and sent electrical charges to places where no man should have to endure. But he had endured. He had told them nothing, and he never would.

They, on the other hand, had told him everything. Their accents, their colloquialisms, the way they smelled, even the way they asked their questions told him they were supposed to be on the same side. They were all supposed to be part of the NATO peacekeeping force, but he suspected this unit had found that the other side paid better.

The funny part, if one could find humor in something this painful, was that while he had secrets, he didn't even have the answers to the questions they were asking, which told him whatever they thought he knew scared the hell out of their puppet masters.

An almost silent sizzle, a little pop, and the locking mechanism on the door fell to the inside of his cell. King looked up into the face of a man he thought he'd never see again. He had an Uzi strapped across his broad shoulders and solid chest.

"Damn, you look like shit," said Robert Fitzwallace, his Scottish brogue thick as he stepped through the door.

They shouldn't have come for him. They shouldn't be here at all.

"Well, you don't look much better, and at least I can blame the way I look on being tortured."

"Smartass."

"I think dumbass is a better descriptor."

"I thought I'd wait until you were back home safe and sound before I pointed that out."

"How'd you find me?"

"I'd say a wee birdie told me, but the truth is you missed a session with Daisy and the lass was upset.

She said something to JJ, who pointed out to me that you wouldn't do that. When I learned you hadn't checked in on time and no one knew where you were, I activated the micro tracker we put on you and here we are."

King chuckled. He had no idea that Cerberus had implanted one of those things on him without his knowledge, but right now, he was damn glad they had. He liked the ex-SAS officer. He was proud, honorable, and never left a man behind. The latter choice had cost him his commission and his pension, even though he held a Victoria Cross. He should have known Fitz would come with his merry band of men who no longer answered to any code other than their own.

Fitz wasn't the only one with a need to be honorable and protect those with whom he served. There was no way King could walk out on his own. He refused to be a burden. They'd need to carry him. Behind enemy lines, that was a death sentence. He wouldn't let anyone else die for him.

"You need to go."

"Good, we're agreed. Sawyer here was certain you would give me grief about it—that honorable American cowboy shit and all."

"No. You need to go, not me. I'm wrecked. I can't walk. I can barely breathe. Leave me and save yourselves."

"Yeah, that's not happening, and you know it,"

said Sawyer, Fitz's right-hand man. "Come on, princess bride, time to go home."

Sawyer rolled out a carry sling on the floor. It took everything King had not to cry out in pain as two other men moved him down onto the sling and lifted him up. Sawyer reached into his pack and pulled out a ball gag, offering it to him.

King chuckled, even though doing so was painful. "You're a sick fuck, Barnes."

Sawyer shrugged. "Yeah, but Rhiannon likes me that way."

"Don't make me laugh, you asshole. And talk to Fitz; this is madness. You'll never get out if you try to take me with you."

"We didn't come all this way to leave empty-handed," said Fitz.

"He asked for volunteers," explained Sawyer. "We had to roshambo to decide who got to come. Me and Fitz? We're in it for altruistic reasons. After all, we're both happily married men. These two chuckleheads think when the subs at Baker Street learn of their heroic deed, they'll be up to their eyeballs in pussy."

"Only because you and Fitz have all the pussy you want or need."

"True enough," laughed Sawyer as Fitz growled. "Now, put the ball gag in; chances are this is gonna hurt."

King realized as soon as they started to move, Sawyer had only been half joking about the ball gag.

He bit down hard enough to leave permanent marks, but they got him out to the chopper that was waiting for them.

The door to each cell they carried him past was open. The others he had heard screaming in the night were gone.

"Don't know who they were or what they were here for, but we figured they had to hate some of them more than you."

King took the ball gag out. "Nobody deserves what they did to me and all the others in there. Nobody."

"Not to worry, lad. There won't be anything but scorched earth after we leave."

As they loaded him into the chopper he could see a large pile of wood, surrounded by what looked like explosives with wires running to more explosives laid along the foundations of the buildings. As they lifted off, King saw the corpses of those who had thought to break him strewn around the ground. The chopper cleared the walls of the fortress or prison—he'd never been sure which it was—and swung back around, firing a missile into the bonfire, and detonating all of the explosives.

Scorched earth, or pussy. King wasn't sure which he preferred more at this moment.

Pussy. Now there was something worth focusing on. He could stay in London at Baker Street to recuperate—maybe have a couple of subs play 'naughty nurse' for him. That was definitely worth living for. His cock twitched. Damn, he'd been worried that his dick's ability to work might have ended up the first casualty of his rendition—apparently not, thank god.

There were men who envied the guys who played at being Doms in some clubs. For a lot of them it was only role play. For men like Fitz, Sawyer, Nigel and a few others, it wasn't something they turned on and off at will. It was an integral part of who they were and how they lived. The Doms he admired were the ones who committed themselves to one woman and made it work.

King wasn't sure he believed in that anymore. He wasn't sure he believed that everyone was entitled to a happily ever after or that any woman would be capable of leading him out of his self-imposed darkness and back into the light… and honestly, after the things he'd seen and done, he wasn't even sure he wanted to go.

A little pinch and King could feel warmth spreading throughout his system. He glanced down at his arm as one of the men who'd carried him from his cell pulled a needle out.

"Nothing bad. It'll just help with the pain and let you sleep on the plane ride until we can get you seen after properly."

He was safe. Or maybe not. They were still, as far as he could tell, in what might be considered enemy territory, but he was a hell of a lot safer than he'd been before the men who had risked their lives to save his—no questions asked—had come to bring him home.

The chopper banked away and sank down beneath the radar to take them to safety as the sun set and the moon began to rise. Taking a deep breath that didn't hurt as much as it had before the medic had given him something, he closed his eyes and let unconsciousness wash over him.

It seemed that the 'scoundrel,' as he'd often been called, had lived through hell and was on his way back home. Maybe it was time to give up being something of a wastrel when he wasn't on a mission. Maybe it was time to listen to Fitzwallace and find a different way. Maybe it was time to take the lifestyle seriously.

~

Baker Street
  London, England
  Present Day

The sub kneeling between his legs had been working on her technique. King had been working on reclaiming his life a little at a time, so they were well-matched.

It had taken a while for him to heal physically.

The mental and emotional wounds had taken a bit longer.

Every sub who arranged a session with him seemed to want to give him back something in return. They saw it as a *quid pro quo* and wanted to service him in some way. They didn't seem to understand that providing them with a safe place to be or giving them something they couldn't get elsewhere made him feel as if a part of the man he had been before still existed. He got as much out of providing them with what they needed as they did. Where were all the subs who wanted a Dom to serve them and give up nothing in return? If they existed, they didn't play at Baker Street.

One of the ways King had begun to reconnect was studying and playing at Baker Street. The physicality of it had been a kind of therapy in and of itself. Using a flogger on a willing sub in such a way that she found peace allowed him to feel as though he was more than just a cold-blooded mercenary. It showed him he was able to provide something more in the world. Granted, it was only a small minority within a very insular world, but still, he usually had more requests for sessions than he could provide.

Any asshole could learn to wield a whip or a flogger, but it took being willing to take control and be in the moment to be a Dom who cared about the sub he was serving. Generally, he ended up with aching muscles and beads of sweat dripping down his body.

To those who would allow it, he provided aftercare, but he rarely requested or needed anything for himself. But for some subs, not providing some kind of sexual service to the Dom who had taken care of them felt as though they'd done something wrong.

Such was the case with Edie. She was a widow and was unsure of her looks or her sexual skills. She had no cause to doubt either. In fact, she'd been on the end of a discipline session for making demeaning remarks about herself more than once. That was something those who ran Baker Street didn't allow. It was hard for Edie to embrace her sexual self. More than one Dom had remarked that if her husband hadn't been dead, he would have been killed by someone at Baker Street. The man had done a number on her self-esteem.

Before Edie could let go and take pleasure from providing pleasure, she needed a firm hand to get her started. King fisted her hair, forcing her mouth down on his cock so that it could reach the back of her throat. The instant he took control, Edie was able to relax and embrace her submissive side.

King couldn't understand how she doubted her abilities. Edie sucked cock better than most. King relaxed back against the chair and groaned in plea-sure, making her smile around his hard length. She slid her tongue along the underside as she swallowed him down. He thrust his hips forward, fucking her mouth. He'd learned a long time ago that he was a visual man. He wanted his subs naked or at least in something very revealing and he loved watching his cock go back and forth between a sub's willing lips.

He thrust deeper and faster while Edie worshiped his cock with her lips, tongue, and mouth. He could feel the all too familiar tingle at the base of his spine as his balls drew up tight. His cock twitched and King pressed her head down against his groin as he spilled himself into her mouth, down her throat, and into her belly.

Like a good girl, she swallowed his load, then ensured he was clean before tucking his cock back into his leathers and expertly lacing up the front. "Thank you, Sir."

"No, thank you."

"I don't mean to be rude, but I'd like to be released so I can get home."

"Do you have someone to see you home?"

"No, but I don't live far, and I know the club's rules about getting home and being safe."

"Good girl."

"Thank you again, Sir. It is always a pleasure to have a session with you."

With practiced skill and grace, Edie rocked back onto her feet, stood, and then headed for the submissives' lounge.

"Some man's going to get himself a real gem," said Fitz, sitting down beside him, tossing a pillow onto the floor, and pointing at it. His wife and submissive, JJ, sank down, laying her head against his thigh so he could stroke her hair.

"What did she do this time?" King asked with amusement.

Everyone at Baker Street knew Fitz preferred to have JJ in his lap. But when he felt she needed to be reminded who was Dom and who was sub, he put her on high protocol, which meant she could only speak when spoken to and sat at his feet instead of cuddled in his lap.

"Oh, just her usual. Too much sass for my liking… and then a bit of a temper tantrum. She knows better, don't you lass?"

"Yes, Master."

She started to rise and all it took from Fitz was a low growl to see her settle back into position.

"You ran that last op perfectly. The client was exuberant in his praise and said they felt without you, they would most likely have lost all of their engineers."

King shook his head. "You have to wonder why the people who say they are fighting to help their fellow countrymen would kidnap engineers who are trying to build safer dams and bridges."

"I know. I swear there's a line item on some of those countries' budgets for a revenue stream derived from kidnapping and ransom. In any event, I wanted to congratulate you on another well-executed op."

"That's great, Fitz; now what do you really want?"

CHAPTER 2

Club Southside
Chicago, United States

Samantha Butler paced back and forth on the sidewalk outside Chicago's newest, and if some were to be believed, best lifestyle club. The world-renowned Baker Street in London had opened up an affiliate club here in Chicago, which was exciting in and of itself. But it wasn't the club she was in need of. Oh, she'd enjoyed Baker Street and Club Termonn up in Inverness. Both could provide a hardworking romance novelist with not only some stress relief, but some great stories and experiences to put in her books—not that she mentioned that to anyone in either club. Anonymity and confidentiality were strictly enforced, but Samantha, or Rook, as her gaming friends called her, made sure no one would ever be able to identify anyone or any place from her descriptions.

The signage was very discreet. Just to the left of the ornate Edwardian-style door there were two plaques. Neither was remarkable. One said, "Club Southside." It was only when you looked at the baroque relief of the sign closely that you realized the "C" was actually a flogger and the lower portion of the "B" was a ball gag. She grinned to herself. Jordan James Fitzwallace had a wicked sense of humor.

Above that sign was another showing a three-headed dog, snarling and snapping, and the word Cerberus. It was the individuals who comprised Cerberus she wished to see. Although… if Club Southside was the same as Baker Street, the men of Cerberus would also be among the Doms at the club.

The building itself had once been an historical landmark, but it had been allowed to fall into disrepair. The story was that the city had wanted to gentrify the neighborhood, not necessarily into a residential one, but more of a place for businesses and entertainment. The classic three-story revival building, which had been a bank at one point in its past, had been built just after the turn of the twentieth century. The city had offered to sell it to Cerberus for next to nothing with the understanding they would bring the building back to its former glory, and now, it was home to Club Southside and Cerberus.

So here she was, switching her weight back and

forth as she waited uncertainly outside the club entrance.

Do I really need Cerberus?

The question kept reverberating in Samantha's mind. Maybe she was just being paranoid. It wasn't outside the realm of possibility. She hesitated and then remembered there was an old cliché that said just because you're paranoid doesn't mean people aren't out to get you.

She was almost certain that someone, a man with a bald head and nicely groomed goatee, had followed her from London. She'd taken a circuitous route from the airport to a different hotel from the one where she'd had a reservation, and checked into the new one under a false name.

Last night had been a nightmare. Nothing had happened but she'd been so frightened that she'd spent the night in the tub, with the door to the bath closed and a chair wedged under the door handle. She hadn't heard anyone trying to get in, but still, she'd been terrified. This morning she'd checked out of the hotel and traveled to Chicago's Union Station, stashing her bags in one of the lockers. All she'd taken with her was her messenger bag, which contained her wallet, phone, and laptop.

She'd found a small diner and had breakfast in the back booth, seated on the side facing the door. Then she'd made her way around Chicago, stopping here or there ostensibly to window shop, but truthfully to look in the window to see if she could spot anyone following her in the reflection.

It was madness. Samantha told herself repeatedly she was overreacting, but she couldn't quite convince herself of that.

Pacing back and forth furiously in front of the building, Samantha muttered under her breath as she glanced up at the door. This was silly. This was Cerberus after all. They probably had all kinds of hidden cameras. Were they inside laughing at her indecision? Was she being paranoid? Even if she was it didn't mean someone wasn't out to get her. She was being stupid. She'd flown across the Atlantic Ocean. Sure, at first it had been just to get away, but get away from what?

The police in England had not outright dismissed her concerns but had implied they didn't necessarily believe her.

"You're a writer, aren't you miss?" the desk sergeant asked.

"What's that got to do with the price of tea in China?" she responded.

"I've heard plenty of people say there's no such thing as bad publicity."

"You think this is some kind of publicity stunt?"

The sergeant shrugged. "It wouldn't be the first time some-one's tried to involve the authorities to give credence to their story. Besides, there's not much we can do about some messages on social media or emails."

"But he knows who I am," she argued.

"Is Samantha Butler your real name?"

"Well, yes, but…"

"Then it wouldn't be that hard to find you, now would it?" The sergeant looked down at his papers. "Unless you have something more substantive, I suggest you get back to your writing."

The break-in had left her spooked and Samantha had boarded the first international flight to America leaving Heathrow. It wasn't until mid-flight that she realized her next move should have been to go to Cerberus in London. But she hadn't been thinking logically. She'd been frightened and wanted to put space between her and whoever seemed to have it in for her.

Samantha continued to pace outside the Cerberus headquarters in Chicago—undecided and agitated. She was acting like a frightened rabbit. She felt foolish. She tried telling herself she needed to find a nice hotel, settle in and get back to work on her book. Of course, she could have done that in England, but she hadn't. From the time she'd entered her little cottage after a day in London, she'd been certain someone else had been there.

She'd gone through the cottage, and nothing seemed out of place, but she couldn't shake the feeling that things had been disturbed and someone had searched her place. Samantha thought about reporting it, but the police had done nothing when she'd taken her concerns about the messages and emails to them. The hairs on the back of her neck had come to attention and she'd known she would not sleep or feel safe in her own home. Someone had taken that from her, and she wanted to know who, why and how to make them stop. She'd hired a cab to take her to Heathrow and taken the first international flight out. Thank god she always carried her passport with her.

After landing at O'Hare, she tried to think about what she knew about Chicago—not much. But then she remembered a notice about the new club that had been emailed to members of Baker Street, letting them know that anyone in good standing had a recip-rocal membership in Club Southside. The previous night spent locked in the bathroom had left her unset-tled. What had her muttering was whether she wanted to go inside for a session, or ask to see someone at Cerberus straight out, or maybe both.

There was a myriad of problems with either scenario. Asking to see someone with Cerberus would mean she really believed, rationally, that she was in danger. She preferred to believe she was simply being distraught but feared that was not the case. Asking for a session was easier to do emotionally, but she was fairly sure, the club would have the same rules as Baker Street about 'appropriate' clothing to be worn on the dungeon floor. Unfortunately, in her haste to leave England, she hadn't thought to bring any.

Although asking for a session was easier, she knew

what she needed was to ask for Cerberus. Maybe if they told her she was just overwrought from the half-written book's impending deadline, she could relax and treat herself to a session with a sexy Dom. What really worried her was that they would find she had cause to be afraid.

Samantha stopped in front of the stairs, confronted the door, and then sighed and walked up. Resting her hand on the doorknob, she took a deep breath, turned the knob, and entered the building.

"Good morning, Miss. The club doesn't open until next week…" said the lovely girl sitting at what seemed to be a reception desk.

"Thank you, but I'm here to see someone at Cerberus."

"Do you have an appointment?"

"Um, no. Do I need one? I'm afraid I've never done this before. I have no idea how it works."

"That's not a problem. Usually people call ahead; we get an idea of what you're looking for and set you up with an initial interview. Your case is presented at a staff meeting. If the team decides to take it, we'll let you know."

"Does it help if I'm a member of Baker Street?"

"I'm afraid reciprocity only extends between the two lifestyle clubs."

"Do I need to leave and call back, or can you make me an appointment?"

"Are you all right?" the girl asked, concerned.

"No. Yes. Oh god, I don't even know anymore. I don't even know what I'm doing here. Am I making any sense at all? Of course not. Look, I won't bother you any longer. If I decide I want to talk to someone, I'll call back. Thank you."

Samantha spun on her heel and headed back across the intimidating stretch of marble that lay between the reception desk and the only door that seemed to offer her an escape.

"Hit the lock, Jen," said a voice from above.

Her eyes traveled up the grand staircase to the source of the deep baritone. Samantha had to remind herself to breathe. The man coming down the stairs looked like some kind of god. Only he wasn't nude, and he wasn't a statue. In some ways he looked like what she imagined Robert Fitzwallace might have when he was a little bit younger. Both men were just the kind of hero her readers liked to see starring in her books.

The man behind the voice was tall, broad shouldered with what looked to be an impressive set of muscular arms, and a sculpted chest. It was encased in a gray, close-fitting Henley, which only showed the distinctive outlines of what she was sure was a spectacular body. The Henley was untucked, and the jeans looked to be Levi's—Samantha loved button flies. Most of her heroes wore Levi's with a button fly and boots. Glancing down, she couldn't help but smile. Sure enough, he—whoever he was—had on cowboy boots. She could easily imagine that shirt concealing a set of washboard abs, and that those jeans contained an impressive cock. The five o'clock shadow dusting his jaw and the windswept hair completed the package.

He reached the bottom of the stairs and strode toward her, extending his hand.

Samantha stepped back. "Do you always lock people inside?" she asked with a bit of an edge. Despite his appearance, the quiet click of the lock had unsettled her.

"Depends on who they are, why they're here, or if I don't want them to leave until I've heard what they have to say. I'm Kingston Coltraine, and if you're a member of Baker Street, you know how to address a Dom. I head up Cerberus here in the States."

Samantha gulped. She had a great many contacts in various intelligence agencies throughout the world. She liked to ensure that her books were accurate. She'd heard the name and some of the stories about him—both in and out of Baker Street.

Straightening her shoulders, she asked, "What makes you think I'm not a Domme?"

"Instinct. I've been in the lifestyle since bootcamp. There's nothing weak about you if that's what bothered you. But you don't have the edge that most Dommes do. If I'm wrong…"

"You're not. Should I sink to my knees in order to apologize?"

"I'm not sure if you're bratting at me or asking sincerely."

"Is there a difference?"

"Definitely bratting; and yes, but we're not in the club per se so the general rules of protocol don't apply."

"I'm sorry, Sir. You're right; I've been trained better than that."

"If you trained at Baker Street, you are under the evil influence of JJ."

Samantha grinned. "There is nothing evil about JJ."

"You're absolutely right. I'm just glad she belongs to Fitz. She is one hell of a woman."

"I do apologize, though. I'm afraid I had a restless night. I thought Adam Wheldon was heading up Cerberus here in Chicago."

"I'm afraid I misspoke. Adam is both the Resident Dom here at Club Southside and is the chief administrator of Cerberus. I'm the bad-tempered sonofabitch who runs ops. He runs the club unfettered. Cases have to be signed off by both of us before we take the client on."

"And if you don't agree?"

"I thought it might be more fun if we took it downstairs to the martial arts cage, but I think Chelsea convinced JJ to make Fitz agree to be the tie breaker."

"I'm sure that would have been his solution as well."

The dreamy Dom with the sexiest voice she'd ever heard chuckled. It was almost as if she could feel the sound caressing her skin in addition to hearing it. "If you believe that, you must not know Fitz. Trust me, his two top guys in Chicago duking it out when they disagree would be right up the Scotsman's alley."

"You might be right about that. But really, I don't want to bother you…"

"I watched you pacing outside. There's obviously something worrying you. Why don't we go up to the conference room and you can tell me what it is?"

Samantha raised her chin. "And if I want to leave?"

"I call Baker Street and find out if we want to perform a friendly intervention." He paused, letting her think a minute. "How about we go into the conference room? I was going to ask Jen to order in some lunch. Nothing fancy, but filling and good."

He was hard to resist, but then most Doms were when they wanted to be and thought they were taking care of someone. Would it be so bad just to let someone see to her needs for just an hour or so?

"All right, but I can pay for my own lunch."

"Let a damsel in distress pay for her own meal? Fitz would have me drawn and quartered."

"I'm no damsel in distress…"

"I'll tell you what, if we take your case, we'll

charge it to client entertainment. If we turn you down, we can go Dutch."

"And what if I decide not to tell you anything?"

He grinned. "Never offer me a challenge. You might not like the way that turns out. Then again, if you're a member of Baker Street, we both might prefer it if you do."

"Has anyone ever told you you're an obnoxious bastard?"

"Quite often. But the first time it happened, I checked with my mother, and she assured me the bastard part, at least, wasn't true."

Samantha turned to Jen. "Is he always like this?"

Jen shook her head. "No. Usually he's worse; he's actually being quite civilized… for him."

"You," he said, pointing to Jen, "behave yourself. And you," he said turning back to Samantha, "pot roast, meatloaf, or club sandwich, a burger, or some kind of salad."

"Pot roast sandwich?"

"Much better than you might think. But if you're unsure, order anything but salad, and you can try mine. If you like it, it's yours."

"Oooh, civilized and gallant," teased Jen.

"Looking to be a demonstration sub for the next discipline training?" he asked sarcastically, but with a hint of a sweet grin.

Jen dropped her eyes "No, Sir."

"Better. Samantha, what would you like to eat?"

"How did you know my name?"

"Facial recognition software. You're Samantha Butler. You're an up-and-coming romance novelist. You're also an avid online game player known as Rook."

"You run facial recognition on everyone wanting to enter your building?"

He shook his head. "No, just the ones who pace up and down the sidewalk talking to themselves." His whole body seemed to soften. "Whatever it is, Samantha, we can help."

"But what if it's nothing?"

"If you thought that were true, you wouldn't be ordering a pot roast sandwich. I'll have the club. Jen, would you mind placing the order?"

"Not at all, Sir." She looked at Samantha. "Are you really Samantha Butler? I just loved that series you set in a club in London. You based that on Baker Street, didn't you?"

"Yes, but I had Fitz and JJ's permission."

"Jen, get us all some lunch. Samantha, you're with me."

As she followed him up the stairs, it was hard not to wonder if she was doing the right thing. Although following perhaps the nicest ass she'd ever seen filling out a pair of jeans couldn't be the wrong thing, could it?

CHAPTER 3

KING

*A*fter showing her to the conference room, King held a chair out for her; Samantha chose another.

So, it's going to be like that. Well, she can run the show for a few minutes. King sat in the chair he'd pulled out originally for her.

"Why don't you tell me what brought you here today?" he asked, trying not to rattle her.

She'd seemed fine downstairs, but upon closer inspection he was pretty sure she hadn't slept much in the past day or so and was frightened. He promised himself he would be patient and professional, but something about Samantha Butler called out to his inner Dom, telling him he needed to take care of her —whether she liked it or not.

"Maybe I just wanted to see the new club," she hedged.

"No," he said, shaking his head. "If that's what you wanted, you'd have been here for the soft opening two nights ago or would have wangled an invitation to the upcoming gala event or the grand opening."

"You don't know that."

"Don't I? I'll tell you what else I know. I know that you paced back and forth outside the building for at least fifteen minutes, looking up at the door over and over again."

"You were watching me."

"You're a beautiful woman. I would think you'd be used to men watching you. Besides, it's the front of my building where you were wearing a groove in the sidewalk. If you'd just wanted to see the club, you'd have come in, flashed your Baker Street membership card, and asked for a private tour. I don't think you're here to see Club Southside at all. I think you're in trouble, or at least very frightened, and you think you need Cerberus."

"You don't know that I need Cerberus."

"You're right," he said, sitting back, "I don't. But I think you think you do. There's a fine tremor in your hand…"

"Maybe I have some kind of nerve degeneration…"

"You don't. If you did, it would be noted in your file at Baker Street, and you keep your nails short, which most likely means you do a lot of typing. If you were having nerve issues, you'd have switched to dictation of some sort."

Samantha glanced down at her hands. He could see her making note of the length of her nails and the barely perceptible tremble.

"What else did your spying on me reveal?"

"Temper, temper, Samantha. Since you asked, I noticed how many times you started up the steps and then turned around. You started to walk away almost as many times. A quick check of the city's hotels revealed that you are not a registered guest at any of them. You came through Customs yesterday morning after a red-eye flight from London, which seems to have been hastily planned. Was it planned at all, or did you just take the first international flight out of Heathrow?"

"Shit. Do I even want to know how you got hold of so much of my personal information?" She shook her head. "I suppose that sounds pretty naive considering I know who you are and as far as I know Cerberus doesn't do any advertising."

"In this day and age, privacy is more of an illusion than a reality. Your run of the mill people can generally be blocked, but corporations with the right kind of people, loads of money and good connections can pretty much find whatever it is they need or want to know."

"Well, I don't like it." She stood up. "Good day, Mr. Coltraine."

"Sit down, Samantha."

"I don't think I will," she said trying to feign outrage.

What did she have to be offended or outraged about? He hadn't said he didn't believe her or thought this was some kind of a publicity stunt. What had her so on edge? She acted as if she thought he was some kind of predator, and she was his prey. If he wasn't careful, she was going to bolt, and something told him that was the last thing he wanted her to do. Time to take control of the situation.

"Sit," he lowered his voice and commanded her.

She hesitated, appearing to fight her first inclination which was to do as she was told, before retaking her seat. *Good.* He'd need to ensure she followed that instinct. Her doing so might save her life.

Where did that thought come from? Instinct… his.

Samantha looked at him as if waiting for some kind of direction. She was a curious girl. Nothing but good reports about her from Baker Street. Several Doms had made note that Samantha had real leanings towards being a SAM—a smart-ass masochist, especially when stressed. King was beginning to believe she was not so much a SAM, but a brat. She wasn't necessarily looking for pain or some kind of punishment, but to get the desired reaction from a Dom.

She was something of an archetypical English beauty—flowing blonde hair, blue eyes, fair complexion and curvy body. When she'd removed her jacket, her figure was revealed to be exactly what he liked. There was strength in her body, but there was also softness and curves where they should be… and she had a great rack. King liked women with curves. He never understood those who starved themselves to be skeletons. The idea of having Samantha under his lash or beneath him when he pounded into her had a lot of appeal.

Her makeup had been carefully done to try and conceal the dark circles under her eyes. She'd pulled her long hair back into a French braid. Her clothing also spoke of her quick decision to leave London. She wasn't prepared for the raw days of late autumn or early winter in Chicago. She had on a pale blue, V-necked sweater, well-fitted jeans tucked into stylish, lace-up-the-front boots. Her only outerwear seemed to be a lightweight, water-resistant coat and a matching scarf and knitted cap in shades of blue, green, and cream.

"Good girl. Let's try again. What brings you to Cerberus?"

She grasped at the hat and scarf a second time.

"Leave them, Samantha and answer my question."

"I don't think I want to have lunch, Mr. Coltraine, and I believe I've made a mistake. If it turns out I was wrong, I can simply go to the police."

The police? That made King's eyebrows knit together, and a lot of alarms go off in his head.

"Why don't you just tell me? If you thought you had enough to go to the cops, you might have, but you're something of a minor celebrity and you don't want the bad publicity."

There was a discreet knock on the door, and Jen slipped in with their sandwiches and a couple of bottles of water. "Either of you want coffee or anything else to drink?"

"No; the bottled water is fine, Jen. Please see that Samantha and I aren't disturbed."

Samantha needs to get used to doing as I tell her. Jen slipped back out as quietly as she'd come in.

"Did it ever occur to you to ask me?" Samantha asked in a snarky tone.

"It did, but then I dismissed it as irrelevant. I think you look like you could use some water. It's funny but most people don't think about dehydration when it's cold. They associate it with heat. But it's just as easy to become dehydrated in the winter as in the summer. Take a bite of the pot roast sandwich and tell me what you think." He shook his head when she started to protest. "Just one bite. If you don't like it, you can have my club. It, too, is excellent."

She ripped open the wrapping paper, lifted the pot roast sandwich and bit into it. Her even white teeth tore into the bread and its contents, but it was the sight of her lips wrapping around the sandwich that made his cock stiffen. King hadn't had this visceral a reaction to a woman in a very long time. He probably shouldn't be feeling that way about a client, but everything about Samantha Butler, aka Rook, went straight to his dick.

"Okay," she said when she swallowed. "This is incredible."

He grinned, hoping she couldn't see how foolishly happy it made him that she liked his favorite sandwich. "I'm glad you like it. Why don't we start with something else. Why the nickname Rook?"

She smiled. "It's the name of the avatar I use in an online role-playing game."

"Why not queen?"

"Do you play chess, Mr. Coltraine?"

"If you can't bring yourself to call me King, how about we revert to club protocol and you can call me Sir."

"Why not throw caution to the wind and call you Master?"

"I haven't earned that title with you yet, but the day is young, and the night is full of possibilities."

Ignoring his quip, she continued, "Most people agree that the queen is the most powerful piece on the board, but she is rarely used aggressively and is often sacrificed. The rook, on the other hand, is considered to be the second most important piece, is often used aggressively, and is rarely sacrificed. I prefer being thought of as the latter."

"I know you're a member of Baker Street…"

"You seem to know a great deal more about me than that."

"I do. I know you're well liked, and I know Adam isn't going to want me to let you leave unless I believe you to be safe here in the windy city. Do *you* believe you're safe, Samantha?"

She leaned forward, almost as if she meant to chide or berate him, but then sat back and took another bite of her sandwich. "This really is good."

"Answer my question. I'm starting to believe those who have labeled you a SAM might be right. I'm coming to the end of my patient indulgence of your behavior. But I think they're wrong."

"I didn't know I'd been labeled."

"Don't take offense, Samantha, Doms make notes about subs to give other Doms better insight into what the sub might need. No confidential information is exchanged. I don't think you're a SAM at all. I do think, though, that you are a bit of a brat."

"A brat? I am not. I think I'd rather be a SAM."

"Do you enjoy pain? That's what a SAM wants. A brat, on the other hand, provokes in order to get a desired result. That end result isn't always painful."

She took another bite of the sandwich, carefully chewing as she seemed to consider what he was saying.

"I never thought of it that way."

King shrugged. "Everything in the lifestyle is

subject to interpretation. One Dom's SAM is another Dom's brat. For me brats can be more challenging as they don't easily express their needs as straightforwardly as a SAM."

Setting the sandwich down, she leaned across the conference table and grabbed one of the bottles of water. King wondered when she did so if she realized she was giving him a rather tantalizing glimpse of her exquisite breasts. They appeared to be more than a handful and he could easily imagine what they might look like clamped, cupped, or just released from a corset. His cock, which had been growing harder and harder behind his fly, was now beginning to throb.

Earlier he'd wanted her under his lash, over his knee, or laid out on her back, her legs spread. Now the vision that came to mind was a naked Samantha on her hands and knees, her brightly colored ass and glistening pussy on full display. He would take hold of her hips and mount her in a single thrust, groaning as he did so and making her gasp as his body connected with her tender backside.

It was a good thing they were seated across the conference table from each other. King was pretty sure Samantha would be able to tell his interest in her had gone from strictly professional to highly inappropriate and very aroused Dom. He had no contract with this woman, not even any kind of understanding, but it was taking all of his vaunted control not to just drag her onto the table, strip her naked, and have at her like a man possessed.

The worst part about this primeval force surging through his body was how much he was relishing it. He'd had sex since they'd patched him up—mentally and physically—after the torture, but mostly it had been oral. He'd been fearful of the feral desires that swirled in his psyche at the thought of actually fucking a woman. King had held back, concerned that he might lose control, but Samantha made him want to indulge—to ravage and worship her. To connect with her in a way he never had before.

"I take it you don't like brats."

"Not at all. I'm considered to be one of the club's best brat tamers. I said they weren't always as easy to care for as a SAM, but then I like a little bit of push/pull. So far, we've talked about sandwiches and lifestyle labels. Why don't we talk about what brought you to Cerberus." He leaned across to cover her hand with his own. "You sought out Cerberus for a reason. What's got you spooked?"

She sat back, withdrawing her hand and King feared he would need to do something to stop her physically. As he was preparing to beat her to the door, she slumped back and took another bite of the sandwich.

Samantha shook her head. "I think you may be right. I may be a brat. I think someone wants to hurt me, and I don't know why. I'm pretty sure I was followed from London, and I'm scared."

CHAPTER 4

SAMANTHA

Samantha inhaled slowly, held it and then exhaled just as slowly. She felt foolish for having just admitted how afraid she was to a man who was more likely than not going to laugh at her. After all, who would want to hurt a romance novelist, especially one who had yet to hit the really big time.

"I'm sorry. This was a mistake. If you'll let me know what I owe you for your time…" she pushed away from the table so she could stand.

"I told you to sit, Samantha. I won't tell you again. Next time there will be consequences for your behavior. Club Southside may not be officially open, but I assure you the dungeon is fully functional."

He had lowered his voice and given it an edge. It was something Samantha noticed that a lot of Doms did. Writers were first and foremost observers. The old saying was to be careful what you said or did in front of an author as everything was grist for the mill. She curled her hands into fists, wanting to resist the urge to do as he commanded. And there was no doubt, she was sure, in either of their minds that Kingston Coltraine had just given her an order. The need to feel safe overrode her indignation and she settled.

"What makes you think someone means you harm?" he asked in a gentler tone.

"That's just it, I don't have a lot to go on. But I received some vaguely threatening private messages on a couple of social media platforms and then some emails that were a little more intense. I suppose they could be interpreted more benignly, but, especially as a whole, they were unsettling. I certainly tried to ignore how they made me feel and had almost convinced myself that it was just my writer's imagination…" she trailed off.

"What happened?"

"I'd gone down to London for a couple of meetings and when I came home… I don't know… it just felt odd, like someone had been there."

"Did you call the cops?"

"Not about the break-in. I did try to talk to them about the messages, but they were pretty dismissive. After that with nothing more than my feelings, I didn't bother. It's not like there was a broken window or furniture tipped over. The house felt like it had been

violated. I know that sounds like an overactive imagination…"

He shook his head. "Not necessarily. Sometimes
there are clues we pick up subconsciously. Just because
you can't identify what tripped your alarm, doesn't
mean it was nothing. You write romance novels, right?"

"I write a combination of romance and suspense,
but yes. I'm not a great literary author."

"Do people buy and enjoy your books?"

"Well, yes."

"Then what else is there? I mean we're forced in
school to read the 'great works' of Dickens, Melville,
Hemingway, but did you enjoy them? I know I didn't.
But I discovered Ludlum, Brown and Patterson when
I was recovering."

"Recovering? Were you ill?"

He chuckled. "No. Not to put too fine a point on
it, I was tortured, which sounds a whole lot more
dramatic saying it out loud than I intended it to. Was
it just the house or the messages or both? Can you
identify the point at which you felt threatened?"

"Not really. I think a growing sense of feeling like
someone means me ill. The tone of the messages had
gotten darker… and then the feeling like someone
had been in my cottage." She stopped, trying to find
the words. "That's the problem. I can't pinpoint any
one thing. I mean people say things on social media
and in emails they'd never ever say in person, much

less follow through on. I showed them to the police; they just dismissed it and told me…"

"It was your vivid writer's imagination and until someone actually did something there wasn't anything they could do." She nodded, and he continued, "I hate that. The problem with stalkers is that a lot of times by the time they actually make their move, it's too late to do anything to prevent it."

He reached for her hand again. It felt warm and comforting. "Do you have them with you?"

"Um, yes, I do. I printed them out."

She had to use both hands to get to the emails and was sorry for the loss of contact. Digging in the messenger bag, she found the emails and private messages. Extricating the stack of papers, she brought them out, handing them to Coltraine. He glanced through them. His face gave away nothing. Samantha was sure the police had been right, and she had spent a lot of money to fly to Chicago only to find out she was an overreactive idiot.

When he placed the sheets of paper on the conference table, she reached across to retrieve them, readying herself to make some excuse and remove herself from the embarrassing situation. He settled his hand over hers again, preventing her from being able to hide the evidence of her vivid imagination.

"Unfortunately," he started.

Here it comes.

But that wasn't what he said as he continued,

looking at her forthrightly. "I can see why the cops didn't think much of it. There's not enough here for them to sink their teeth into. But I can also see why you thought you were being threatened. For the record, I think you're right."

For a moment Samantha stopped breathing. "You do?"

Coltraine nodded. "I do. Do you have any idea who sent them?"

"No. I don't even know for sure it's the same person. The return email isn't the same, and a friend who's pretty good at these things said they came from different servers."

"Both of those are easy enough to do. But if you look at the phrasing, it's very similar throughout the emails, and this one phrase…" He pointed at one of the pieces of paper. "…'you are known to me in all ways,' shows up in all of them. If it was something like 'I'm coming after you,' or 'You belong to me,' it would be one thing. Those are fairly common, but his phraseology is strikingly similar in all of them and spot on in that one.'

Samantha didn't bother to try and hide her look of shock. The police had been dismissive and made her feel silly.

"You figured that out? Just by glancing through them? The police didn't and neither did I, to be honest."

"Neither you nor the cops are trained to find

things that connect quickly. I worked in intelligence, where being able to spot patterns can keep you alive. And that instinct that's been telling you you're in danger? It's one that operatives depend on to keep them from getting killed."

"In a weird way, I'm glad you don't think I'm just some emotionally overwrought person, or that maybe this was some kind of publicity stunt to increase sales."

"Is that what the cops said?"

"Said? The desk sergeant at the police station didn't make an outright accusation, but there was a heavy implication that he thought that was the case. I didn't appreciate his indifferent attitude and so when I thought my cottage had been broken into, it was very distressing so I just kind of panicked and wanted to get out of England."

"If this was a publicity stunt," he said, "it would be illegal to involve the cops. But for the record, I don't believe that at all."

Samantha gave a half-hearted smile. "I'm not sure I wouldn't have liked it better if you had agreed with the cops back in England. I wish to hell it was a publicity stunt."

Coltraine cocked his head to one side. "Why?"

"Because then you could give me a choice between a discipline session for wasting your time or giving up my membership."

He chuckled. "I take it you'd opt for discipline?"

She nodded. "Not to worry, Samantha, if that's what you need, we can provide that as well." She looked up and saw the warm embers of desire lurking in his eyes. "Can I keep these?"

It took her a moment to come back to reality. "Yes, of course. I can print out more if I need to."

"Good. Where are you staying?"

"My bag is in one of the lockers at Chicago's Union Station. I wasn't sure where I was going to stay."

"Let me have the key. I'll send Jen to go get your bags for you. Is there anything you need in addition to the bags?"

"Not really. I thought I'd try to figure out my next move before I got anything else."

"Your next move, until I tell you otherwise, is to do as you're told. As in London, Cerberus here in Chicago not only has private playrooms, but we have a couple of safe rooms with enhanced security. We're going to move you into one of those."

"Cerberus is going to take my case?"

Coltraine nodded. "Officially, I have to discuss it with Adam, but he and his wife took a bit of a vacation and got snowed in, so I'd rather not bother him. You'll be safe here with us. I'll make sure of it. Don't worry, Samantha, we'll keep you safe and find this asshole."

For the first time in over a week, Samantha felt herself relax and with that came tears. Coltraine was up, out of his chair and around to her before she knew what was happening. He was fast, quiet and graceful. Pulling out a handkerchief, he dabbed gently at the tears rolling down her cheeks before handing it to her.

"I'm sorry. I don't normally just burst into tears."

"I suspect you aren't 'normally' stalked by anyone. From here on out, you don't leave this building without my permission."

"Or Adam's…"

"No. My case; my permission. I know the building is secure. You're a member of Baker Street. You know the kind of security clearances we put on members. You're here for the duration."

As sexy and comforting as she found him—which in and of itself was a weird combination—Samantha found herself bristling at his domineering manner but ultimately ended up laughing.

"Care to share the joke?"

"I was about to take affront at you dictating orders to me and then the part of my brain that was thinking reminded me that you're a Dom. I would, however, remind you that I'm not your sub and am in fact the paying client."

He stood and looked down at her with a grin that she couldn't decide was sexy or a bit evil—maybe a little of both.

"You do realize you are in a secure lifestyle club with a Dom who is known to be a brat tamer. I'm warning you right now; don't try me. You are under the protection of Cerberus, and we take that shit seriously."

"Are you trying to tell me I have no choice in any of this?"

"I'm telling you that your choice at the moment is between whichever one of the two suites we keep as 'safe houses' are open."

"What am I supposed to do for food?"

"Each of the suites has a bunch of different restaurants' take-out menus. You can either give us a list of things you like or don't like and we can order for you, or highlight specific items you'd like to have. The alternative is we do have a full kitchen so if you like to cook, we can order in food."

"Will I be here by myself at night?"

He smiled, "No, Samantha. I will be here, and we have a state-of-the-art security system. Each of the suites was built so that the bath could be used as a panic room. If the alarm goes off, or a member of Cerberus tells you to or you just feel frightened, you go in there, lock the door, and hit the red button. That will alert the team and the cops that there's trouble. You're safe here."

"What about when the club opens?"

"Hopefully we'll have found this guy before then. If not, then when the club is open, you're restricted to the third floor where the suites and the Cerberus offices are located."

"What about your vaunted security clearances to become a member?"

"We don't want anyone to know where you are. Period." He must have seen the downtrodden look on her face. "What?"

"What if I need something only the club can provide?" her voice dropped to a barely audible whisper as she fidgeted with her hands.

Oh god, did she really want to go there? Did she really want to admit to this man she knew little to nothing about that she could really benefit from some kind of relief session. There were times when she was bound in an intricate shibari pattern, that the binding made her feel safe. Other times, she needed some kind of physical impact to allow her to break through her walls and feel and get out of her system whatever it was that seemed to be holding her captive. It was weird that most normal people she knew found neither being bound nor being struck with a whip or a flogger empowering and freeing.

Coltraine leaned down, covering her hand with his. "If you mean an orgasm, there are plenty of toys to be found in the safe suite. If you mean a session, I can provide you with that when the club isn't open."

He was a Dom? Of course, he was. Hadn't she heard that all of the members of the Cerberus team in London were in the lifestyle? Wasn't Kingston Coltraine everything she wanted in a Dom? The man was gorgeous and seemed incredibly powerful—both physically and mentally.

"What if I want another Dom to work with me?" she asked, withdrawing her hand all the while hoping he wouldn't allow it.

He didn't. He didn't make a big deal of the fact that he could hold her in place, but he made his point before releasing her hands and straightening. "I'm afraid that won't be possible."

"Why not?"

"For one thing I caught your case, which makes me the agent in charge; and for another, I'm not inclined to share. Finish your sandwich," Coltraine said as he returned to the other side of the table. "When we're done, you'll give your locker key to Jen. She'll go and get your things and bring them back to you. In the interim I'll take you on a tour of the third floor, and you can pick which room you want and get settled in."

"I won't have much to settle in with until Jen gets back."

"True enough, but I have some paperwork to do for your case. You're a writer, write. There's a desk with a proper chair and lighting. If you want a printer, we can put one in there for you."

"What kind of paperwork," she asked suspiciously.

"Whenever we take on a client, we have them sign certain documents that allow us to do our jobs. In addition, there's a client intake sheet. I'll fill it out and you'll need to sign it. It won't take long, but it'll let us spell out things between us."

"Okay. You said the room has an attached bath?"

"Absolutely. If you want to take a shower and put something else on, we have all kinds of things that can be worn by people visiting the club."

Samantha laughed. "Somehow a corset and thong doesn't sound all that comfortable. Any chance there's a pair of sweats somewhere?"

Coltraine grinned. "Killjoy."

"Jackass," she returned with little rancor.

They finished lunch making the kind of polite small talk people close to being strangers made— filling the empty space with nothing that could be held against them. When Jen knocked on the door, it was difficult to tell who was more relieved—Coltraine or Samantha.

"You said you had an errand for me?" Jen asked.

Coltraine extended his hand to Samantha, "I need the key to the locker."

"I can get my things…"

"No. You can't. If someone followed you here or if they saw you duck into Union Station they could be waiting for you to return. They don't know Jen; they won't even give her a second glance in terms of being connected to you. How distinctive is your bag?"

"Not very. It's a simple weekender-type bag in

black. Why do you ask? It'll be the only bag in the locker."

"But if someone is following you and they've seen the bag, being unique could make them take a look at Jen even if she is being nondescript."

Samantha nodded and handed Coltraine the key.

"Jen, do me a favor and wear some kind of over-sized jacket and a hat. Try to call as little attention to yourself as possible. I know you're gorgeous and hard to forget, but see if you can just blend in."

She snapped him a jaunty salute. "Blending in, Sir."

He chuckled. "Keep your eyes open. If you even get a hint you're being followed, head back to Union Station and I'll have a team pick you up."

"Why don't I go home first, put on something really dull, and take my own bag. Then I can slip in, grab her stuff and put it in my bag. I'll grab a latte on the way out so if anyone saw me go in, everything looks the same and I have a reason to have gone inside in the first place."

"Good idea. Just be aware of everything and everyone around you and be careful."

"Will do," Jen said with a grin. Turning to Samantha she said, "Anything I can pick up for you?"

"A latte would be great," said Samantha.

"In that case, ask King to make you one. He makes the best flavored lattes."

Jen turned and left them alone.

Somehow, he'd lost her at Union Station. He'd followed her, but he'd lost her in the crowd. He'd waited for her to return, not knowing what else to do. She was proving to be a far more elusive prey than he'd thought when he'd started the game.

He knew she liked to play online games. Knew she was considered to be one of the best, but he knew better. She thought she was so smart, but she wasn't. As he'd told her, he knew her in all ways, and that would prove her undoing. What she wrote made a mockery of relationships that were right and proper.

The stalker watched as a woman of Samantha's approximate height and build headed to the storage lockers. He followed, never giving himself away, blending in with the people who moved around the large space—coming and going and never knowing he was there.

She opened the locker, but instead of taking out the bag inside, she opened the bag she had slung over her shoulder, set it down and emptied the contents of the locker into the bag she had set on the floor.

She stopped to get one of those fancy coffees and he fell in behind her. At one point the woman looked back, but dismissed him as a threat, but continued to watch everything and everyone around her. Neither she nor anyone else was aware that he was stalking her; that he would be the predator to her prey. She turned into an alley and picked up her pace. Did she sense he was following her? There had been a few close calls—like at Samantha's cottage—but he had managed to elude her.

This was his chance; she was alone. He could eliminate his obsession by killing her, letting her blood wash away all the sinful thoughts and deeds that threatened to consume him when he thought of her. Did none of her adoring fans understand that all of her titles were secret signals to him? At first they had been seductive and alluring, but then they had turned to ridicule and scorn. Silently he caught up to her, making his move, wrapping his left arm around her neck while he pumped two slugs into her back, one of which should have hit her heart.

She slumped down with the same muffled sound as the gun with the silencer. Blood mixed with the rain that had begun to fall. He flipped her onto her back. He wanted her to see, as her life slipped away, that it was him so that she would know that he was the victor in their game.

He stared into the face of the woman beneath him. It wasn't Samantha. Shock pulsed through him like the blood pumping from her arteries. He wanted to rage, wanted to shout, wanted to shoot her ten more times...but all he did was rise to his feet and back away.

It seemed the game wasn't over just yet.

CHAPTER 5

KING

Once Jen had come and gone, King and Samantha finished their lunch in companionable silence, broken only by random small talk. He didn't need Samantha picking up on how attracted he was to her, aside from his small nudges about providing her with a session. He reminded himself that she was a client first but might well benefit from the steadying hand of a Dom. The last thing she needed was to catch a glimpse of the wolfish predator he was working hard to hide.

She was truly lovely, and he lost all respect for the unattached Doms at Baker Street. One of those idiots should have collared her a long time ago. He meant to ensure their loss was his gain. She was strong and something of a brat, but then, he liked strong-willed brats. They were a lot more fun to tame.

King had been the subject of plenty of women's,

not to mention sub's, fantasies and plots. For the most part he didn't mind fueling the first, but he foiled the latter every single time. Those who wanted to fantasize were free to do so, but he made it clear that the fantasy was all they got. He'd wanted nothing more committed than a little role play and sexual satisfaction. Somehow with Samantha, he already knew he wanted so much more.

It really was ridiculous. How many times had he teased the other members of the Cerberus team for falling head-over-heels for a sub or any woman. The idea of insta-love or love at first sight had always seemed absurd to him. He was quite certain he would be eating his words the next time he was in London or when any of the London team ventured here to Chicago.

He hadn't mentioned it to Samantha but the escalation in the emails was worrisome. The first email was fairly dispassionate but had escalated to the stalker's belief that she belonged to him and then that she had done him wrong. The last one Samantha had given him had been an outright threat that the cops should have taken seriously. But still there was no reason to think that Jen would be in danger.

Fortunately, King's plan for Samantha was straight forward and he believed simple to execute. Samantha would stay here in one of Cerberus' safe rooms, he would become her Dom, and he would save her. The only real wrinkle he could see in his plan was that she might not be onboard for the whole King becoming her Dom thing. He meant to present it as a way for people to accept her as part of the club while limiting her contact with others.

It was a good plan. Now all he had to do was get Fitz to sign-off on it. The problem with trying to enlist Adam's help was that he wasn't here for the next few days, and he tended to get all caught up in the whole informed consent thing. On the other hand, Fitz would understand King's need to tie the relationship, and his new sub, down—figuratively if not literally.

When she was finished with her sandwich, King pushed back from the conference table having gotten his unruly cock to settle down with the promise of things to come.

"How about I take you upstairs and show you around?"

"Don't you have to have Adam sign off on taking my case?"

"Not necessarily. I thought I'd just run it by Fitz. I can do that first if you like."

Glancing at his watch, King decided it should still be early enough to call Fitzwallace and placed the call.

"King. What do you want?" King smirked to himself as the call was answered. The Scotsman was not overly effusive in his greetings to begin with, and he didn't appreciate his time with JJ being interrupted.

"Let me get straight to the point. Samantha Butler is here in Chicago. She thinks she has a stalker, and so do I."

Out of the corner of his eye, he saw her tremble, and laid his hand over hers. The fact that she didn't withdraw her hand almost made him giddy, which was an entirely over-the-top reaction.

"Why didn't she come to us here in London? Is the stalker there in the States?"

"Unknown. She didn't come to you because the cops made her feel foolish. But she got spooked and bolted to America. The first plane out landed her here in Chicago. I watched her pace outside our office for more than twenty minutes before she came in."

"What do you think and what do you need from me?"

"I think she's being stalked. Did the guy follow her? As I said, I don't know but I'm not inclined to take chances with her safety. I'm putting her up in one of our secure suites until we figure this out."

"Did you talk to Adam?"

"I don't know that there's a need to. It's pretty obvious she needs looking after. Besides, Adam took Chelsea for a little one-on-one time. I guess his trip to Colorado last New Years turned out to be more of a work thing than an anniversary celebration. Unless you think it's absolutely necessary, I'd rather leave him out of it until he gets back."

"Probably a good idea. Just make sure we keep her safe. If something happens to her, JJ will be pissed. She loves the books Samantha and Sage Matthews write. I haven't read one myself, but I have to say I love the mood they put JJ in. It's a boon that they're both members. Damn police," snarled Fitz. "What were they thinking?"

"They let Samantha know they thought it was some kind of publicity stunt."

"If that's what she was looking for, why not leak it to the press?" grumbled Fitzwallace.

"Exactly," replied King.

"Keep me advised, and you're authorized to do whatever you need to do to keep her safe, regardless of the cost." He paused. "I'm sure you understand my drift. Samantha can be a bit of a brat." He chuckled. "I'd give anything to watch the two of you tangle."

"Message received."

King ended the call, relieved to find Samantha appeared to be relaxed and smiling. King didn't know anyone at Baker Street, Club Southside, or Cerberus who didn't envy JJ and Fitz's relationship. It was something most people aspired to. The Scotsman might be fierce, but he was deeply and passionately in love with his wife, and there was little he wouldn't do to make her happy. The feeling and commitment were mutual.

"He's nuts about her," said Samantha, echoing his thoughts.

"He is, and she feels the same way about him. Come on, let's go up to the third floor and I'll show you around."

He led her out of the conference room and over to the only elevator in the building. It was small and vintage and went from the basement all the way to the top floor, where the security suites and the American headquarters of Cerberus were housed.

"This is beautiful," Samantha said.

"It is and it's original to the time period, but not to this building. We had to create a special shaft for it to work in. As you saw earlier, there's a staircase from the first floor to the second. There is also another set of stairs from the first floor down to the basement. The only way to the third floor is on this elevator and to go down into the basement or up to the third floor, requires a special key code. There is, by design, no staircase to the third floor."

King didn't bother to tell her about the hidden staircase at the back of the building that was only accessible with fingerprint and retina identification and led to a concealed door in the alley. It was only to be used for emergencies, and no one in the club knew about it… just those with Cerberus.

He opened the grill to the vintage elevator and ushered Samantha inside. She ran her hand over the beautiful wood paneling. Pulling the grill and then the door shut, King punched in the code and the elevator began to ascend to the third floor. The doors opened into a massive bullpen with desks, computers, and the normal office set up. He took her on a brief tour, showing her both his and Adam's offices.

To the side of the office was a separate hallway that led around behind it to the two security suites, as well as a small armory.

"We have a weapons cache on each floor, just in case we're attacked and have to defend ourselves," he answered her unasked question.

He unlocked the door to the first safe room, which was rather stark and utilitarian. It was comfortable enough and was decorated and appointed adequately but was not set up for a long-term stay with the inhabitant's comfort in mind.

"That one will do in a pinch and was actually set up when we realized we'd be better off with two. I think you'll like the original one better."

King led her to it, opening the door with a bit of a flourish to reveal an interior which was decked out for royalty and other heads of state. It was almost twice the size of the other suite and had an enormous king-size bed and a bath with a huge tub and a separate shower that looked big enough for three or four people.

There was a walk-in closet which housed a cabinet full of all kinds of toys and implements—everything for the discerning kinkster.

He loved how expressive her face was as she took it all in. He showed her around the suite, directing her attention to the huge round window that looked out over Lake Michigan and had an inviting window seat. He wondered if she noted the wall next to it with a large St. Andrew's cross constructed within a wheel. If desired, it could be rolled in front of the window and secured there. He had a momentary flash of an image of Samantha bound naked to the cross with his marks laid across her major muscle groups.

The other large window was not round; nor was it set up for play. It did have a seating area with a recliner set up in front of it.

"The glass is bullet and tornado proof. Even if someone could get up here, they couldn't get in. I'm not sure even a missile would shatter the windows on this floor."

"It's gorgeous."

He nodded. "Good. I'm glad you like it."

"It is going to be okay, isn't it?

"You have my word on it."

"But what if it isn't and one of us gets killed?"

"Then the one of us who is dead won't care much about it."

She spun on her heel and glared at him. "That's not funny."

"Maybe, but it's also true and I have no intention of letting anything happen to either of us. I promise you'll be safe, and we'll find whoever is doing this to you and see that they're prosecuted and put in jail."

"But if they're British citizens…"

King was unsure if she didn't want to believe she was being stalked or if she didn't believe they could keep her safe. She was wrong on both counts.

"It only matters when we have them arrested. If they're in England, we have a Cerberus office in London that has contacts with the legal authorities over there. If they're here in the States, we have the same kind of contacts with the Chicago Police Department. Regardless of what happens or where it happens, you came to the right place. When I look at these emails, there is no doubt in my mind that you have a stalker, and he's escalating. You tried telling the cops in England and they blew you off. Why? I'll never know. But you now have Cerberus on your side. We've been known to bring entire governments to their knees, so your stalker doesn't stand a chance."

Samantha sighed and seemed to try to force herself to relax. "Thank you. I probably should have stayed in London and gone to Baker Street. But… have you ever had the hair on the back of your neck stand up?"

"More than once, and each and every time, listening to that little voice inside my head has kept me from losing it. So as far as I'm concerned, you did the right thing."

She had been facing the window, gazing out at the

view. Samantha turned and looked at him. "You really do believe me, don't you?"

"I don't understand why the cops didn't. I'll reach out to some of our people in London and see what I can find. I'm going to assume this would be the suite you'd prefer."

"Yes, please. And thank you. Thank you for lunch, for believing me, and for giving me a place to stay where maybe I can sleep."

"Did you sleep at all last night?" he asked gently.

"Not really. I ended up locking myself into the bathroom in the hotel, wedging a chair under the doorknob, and sitting up in the tub. I'd nod off every now and again and would just jerk awake. I'm pretty knackered and everything aches."

He nodded. "In that case, I want you to take a shower. The one in here has a steam option. Do that and let it open up everything. I'll run you a hot bath in about ten minutes and you can go straight from the shower to the tub. Before the water starts to cool, I'll get you out and tuck you into bed for a nice long nap. We can have dinner when you wake up and then you can go back to bed. I want you to know, you will not be alone."

"There's only one little problem with your plan."

"What's that?"

"If you're getting me out of the tub, you'll see me naked."

"That's not a problem."

"It is for me."

"No, it's not. Your file says you have an exhibitionist streak a mile wide. Besides, there have to be some perks in my line of work. Seeing you naked is one of them."

"What if I don't want you to? Better yet, what if I tell you if you get to see me naked, I get to see you naked?"

He closed the distance between them, sliding his hand beneath her golden tresses to cup the nape of her neck so she could feel his strength, before lacing his fingers through her mane and squeezing his fist closed around her hair and tugging her head back.

"If you want to see me naked, Samantha," he said, dropping his voice down low, his mouth hovering over hers, "all you have to do is ask. But if I get naked, I'm going to want to do more than look."

CHAPTER 6

SAMANTHA

*D*anger! *Danger! Danger! Coltraine was right. Normally, she was an exhibitionist, but becoming a full-time author at home had been a challenge. She was good at time management, but the healthy eating habits she'd once had were gone. Stress about deadlines, imposter syndrome and whether her books would sell and then continue to sell had caused her to reach for a lot of fattening comfort foods and plenty of M & M's. She'd added about twenty-five pounds to her once svelte frame.*

All of the warning bells and instincts that had warned her of a stalker went off. Not that she thought Coltraine was a stalker, but she knew in every fiber of her being that getting mixed up with him was a bad idea. She also knew that she'd never wanted anything more than to have him lower his head and kiss her.

He thought a hot, steamy shower and a long soak in a tub would make her feel better? He was so wrong.

What she needed was this man right here, right now. At her look, and the tension arcing between them, he hesitated only a moment longer before fusing his lips to hers, teasing and taunting as heat and arousal surged through her system. He was seducing her, enticing her, arousing her—and she welcomed it all.

Coltraine tilted her head back, moving it into the position he wanted as he ran his tongue across the seam of her lips, provoking and teasing her into parting them, so he could more fully invade her mouth. Samantha moaned, not because he was hurting her, but because it had been so long since someone had made her body come alive in the way he did.

It had been over a year since she'd allowed anyone to touch her sexually. She'd asked for and received stress relief sessions at the club and usually the man tending to her needs wanted to be repaid in kind, which seemed only fair. Sometimes it felt a little too clinical; a little too business-like, but at least it allowed her to reset and get back to work.

Ever since she'd been introduced to Sage Matthews, Samantha had done everything to mimic her work ethic and drive. Sage had become something of a mentor, and Samantha had no intention of not taking full advantage of Sage's largess. Doing so had paid off in steadily increasing royalties on her books. But it had negatively impacted not only her social life, but it had also all but killed off her sex life. She found far more distraction and relief in playing online video games with people she most likely would never meet.

Samantha had first been introduced to the lifestyle by her friend Mazie. They'd played on the same team in the online and real-life versions of Castle Reign, a popular video game. At one point Mazie had talked her into coming with her and Holden, Mazie's husband, to Baker Street. At first it had been all she could do not to run for the hills, but as the couple showed her around, she had become intrigued. Samantha hadn't done anything particularly exciting or sexy that night, but she'd certainly seen a lot and had talked to a lot of the subs about what they got out of it. She'd been surprised to find the only consistency to be found among the women who identified as 'submissive'—either in general or to just one man—was that the lifestyle allowed them to let go of their everyday cares and find solace in their submission.

One of the women she'd met that night was the owner of the place, Jordan Fitzwallace. No one had ever called JJ a wall flower or accused her of being anything less than a strong, proud, assertive woman who didn't take shit from anyone, including her imposing husband. JJ understood the conflict Samantha was dealing with and offered to allow her to attend several more evenings as her personal guest and then if she was interested, to attend the training course for submissives.

JJ later told her that lifestyle clubs were only as

good as their people and finding the right people for the club was always a struggle. Samantha had been fascinated with everything, most especially the people —Doms and subs alike. She was also impressed by the training given to the submissives, and surprised, as well, to find the Doms went through far more rigorous training than their sub counterparts.

Samantha had learned that she tended to let her mind wander and not be present and in the moment with people. She always attributed it to being a writer, but most Doms wrote it off as arrogance, boredom, or not caring about her partners. Coltraine snapped her back to attention when his hand snaked up under her sweater, and he trailed his fingers across her breasts. She wasn't expecting that. She had hoped the bulky sweater would hide the evidence of her arousal. His fingers tightened around her nipple and gave it a firm pinch, which made her gasp.

His mouth plundered hers, his tongue surging in over and over to tangle with hers. Samantha had never been one to drink heavily and had never done drugs. She imagined the way Coltraine kissed was similar to being high or drunk. He made her understand why people were attracted to both and found it hard to give them up. As she yielded and focused on Coltraine, his kisses morphed from seductive to dominating in the space of a heartbeat.

Samantha understood this wasn't just some random

kiss, this was a declaration of intention to possess her in a way no man had done before. She put her hands on his chest and pushed, but he didn't yield. She fought to free her mouth, but he continued to kiss her breathless.

"Stop it," she managed to whisper.

"No. If you really want me to stop either use your safeword…"

"You don't know my safeword…"

"It's *check*."

He hesitated a moment and when she said nothing, he grinned in a way that reminded her of the way dragons must have looked at their virginal sacrifices. Only he was no dragon and she sure as hell wasn't a virgin.

This was what had so attracted her to the lifestyle. She could be as strong as she needed to be in her daily life, but during the time she played in the club, she didn't have to be strong, didn't have to be in charge. She could just be.

Again, he waited, and she didn't have the courage to use her safe word. It wasn't that she was afraid of him. It was more that she felt safe with him, and that, in and of itself, was frightening. She felt safer than she had at any time in the past several days. When she said nothing, he lowered his head and covered her mouth with his again. This time, she didn't acquiesce or give into her own need—and it was there, a need strong and so, so seductive. It would have been easy just to sink into her own submission. Instead, she bit his lip.

Lifting his head, he responded, coolly, "You might want to rethink how you behave with me. I've tamed more than my fair share of brats. I am a whip master, which means I can get you to relax and orgasm under my lash, but I can also turn your ass a fiery crimson with my hand to teach you to mind me."

"Isn't the goal of a good Dom to teach a brat to behave for anyone?" Samantha wasn't sure why she was so intent on taunting him.

"Depends on the Dom and what his goals are. Frankly, unless it's in the matter of your safety, I don't give a rat's ass if you submit to anyone else but me. I will require that you are respectful, but as far as I'm concerned, you never need to kneel to anyone else again."

"What do you mean by that?"

He chortled. Why was it that so many Doms had the most devastating chuckles? Coltraine's was warm, seductive, and far too effective.

"Precisely what you're afraid I mean."

She lifted her chin—although whether it was defiantly or just stubbornly she was no longer sure.

"I'm not afraid of you."

Again, with the deep, rumbling sound of amusement. Apparently, he found great enjoyment in her consternation.

"Physically? I have no doubt, but mentally and emotionally is another matter entirely."

"You're an arrogant jerk. I want someone else assigned to my case."

"No."

"What do you mean no?"

"No one else will be assigned to your case."

"You can't just arbitrarily…" she started and had to stop as she felt the tears beginning to well. She hated when her emotions got so out of hand that she began to weep. It was such a weak, ineffective response to things.

"You'll find that I can."

He looked deep into her eyes and in the end, she couldn't hold his gaze and so lowered her own as he took her mouth and began to kiss her with an unbound passion that drew her like a moth to a flame. She gave herself up to his heat, not caring if he singed her wings or even sent her up in a great plume of fire.

Finally, he raised his head and stared down in her eyes. Those were not the eyes of the professional who had greeted her this afternoon. No, this was some kind of primitive beast that meant to claim her as his own.

"Why?" she whispered.

"Because I want to, and even more than that, I think you want me to. You need someone to take control. That's what attracts you to the lifestyle in the first place. To succeed in your chosen profession, you have to be strong and resilient. Only there are times that all of it—the work, the success—gets to be too much and there's no one you can turn to. Instead, you turn to the club. You keep it professional and yourself aloof. You find some relief, but never the solace or peace you're looking for. I can give those to you, Samantha; I want to."

She shook her head.

"That's not your safe word," he said with amusement. "What do you need, Samantha?"

She couldn't. Not here; not now. Someone was after her. Coltraine agreed with her. He assured her she was safe, but was she? She'd never felt more out of control in her life. She needed to get that control back, not hand it over to a man she barely knew.

"You can't find it in yourself to ask, can you?" he said, kissing her softly. Samantha shook her head. "That's all right. I won't make you ask, but I can give you what you need. Can you at least trust me to give it to you?"

She opened her eyes and tilted her head back. She still couldn't verbalize it—couldn't admit out loud what she needed, but she knew he understood. She nodded.

Coltraine pulled her close and his mouth captured hers once again, literally stealing her breath away. His cell phone buzzed and rang. He ignored it and kept kissing her, showing no indication that he'd even heard it. The caller either gave up or left a voice mail as the phone went silent and still his tongue danced with hers, flooding her being with arousal. The phone vibrated again, but this time the ringtone was Wagner's *Ride of the Valkyries*.

Everything in Coltraine stopped and he reached for his phone. "Sorry. I can't ignore this one. That ringtone means there's an emergency."

He kissed her again before raising his head. He didn't turn away or even let her go. He merely brought his phone up to his ear, while leaving his other arm wrapped around her middle, holding her close and allowing his cock to throb between them. Samantha was surprised she didn't feel annoyed or at least let down. He wasn't just being distracted. The first time the phone went off, he had ignored it completely. She was kind of surprised he'd been able to do that and had chosen to focus on her instead.

"Are you sure?" he said into the phone. "There's no chance it could be anyone else?"

[*Indistinct talking*]

"Of course not. I understand. We'll get someone down there to identify the body. I don't want to put her family through that. We'll bring the fingerprints we have on her. Please don't call anyone else. I'd rather we broke the news to them."

[*Indistinct talking*]

"I understand that. Someone will be at the

morgue as quickly as possible. Thank you for letting me know."

He ended the call. Even though he'd held her close, she could feel his withdrawal.

"That was the police," he started. "More specifically a contact of ours within the police. They found Jen."

Everything inside Samantha went cold. She shook her head and tried to pull away, but Coltraine held fast.

"No," she said, shaking her head.

"I'm afraid so. She was killed. Two shots, close contact, one straight through the heart. I need to get someone down there…"

"You should go."

"No, I shouldn't. Someone needs to stay with you, and I'm already here. I'll get Seth or Royce to go. We're going to have to notify her family, but I'd rather we had as much information as possible. I know we were on the edge of something…"

Samantha realized then that she'd been wrong when she'd felt the Doms with whom she had sessions received nothing more than a blow job from her in return. It had felt a bit one-sided. She'd gotten the emotional high and release she needed. But she always felt as if all they got was a physical alleviation of their hard-on. Until this moment, she hadn't realized that as much as she needed to give up control, they had an equal need to take it.

"Don't. That edge will be waiting. This is more important." For the first time, she initiated physical contact with him, by wrapping her arms around him and resting her head on his chest. He leaned his cheek against the top of her head. "I'm so sorry for the loss of your friend."

"It shouldn't have happened."

"No, it shouldn't have, but you aren't responsible."

"I sent her."

"But he killed her. There was no way you could have known. You said yourself he was escalating…"

"More than enough reason not to send her."

Samantha brought her head up, looking him square in the eye. "No. She wasn't dressed to look like me, it was broad daylight, and she was trained to do this kind of thing."

"You don't know that…"

"Don't I? You would never send one of your people, especially a woman, into danger or any situation you didn't feel they could handle. If anyone should feel guilty, it should be me."

"Why you?"

"Because it's very possible that the killer shot her thinking she was me."

"This is not your fault," he said in a very dominant voice.

"I know," she said gently. "It's not my fault any more than it is yours. There's only one person responsible and that's the sonofabitch who decided to make me his victim. Only we're not going to let him do that, are we?"

He smiled down at her. "I knew there was more than a brat lurking behind those big blue eyes. And no, he won't get away with it, but your part in this is to do as you're told and stay safe."

"You aren't actually so delusional or arrogant enough to think one kiss is going to tame the brat, are you?"

The smile spread and the clouds of guilt and grief began to lift from his eyes. "No."

He kissed her briefly and lightly but with even more feeling. Something between them had shifted and they both knew it.

CHAPTER 7

KING

*K*ing had been wrong about her. He'd known there was something far more alluring than just the brat she presented to the world. He'd felt a deep and almost immediate connection to her as if she was the piece he'd always been missing.

"I need to…" he started.

"Do whatever it is you need to do. We are in a perfectly secure building. I'll grab a quick shower while you head on into the office—"

"And miss the chance to see you naked? That's not happening, baby."

She rolled her eyes. "Fine. Stay and look all you want, but I really could use something else to put on. I've had on these clothes for almost two days. Does the club keep anything I can wear?"

"I'm sure I can find you a corset and a thong…"

She laughed, and realized when he smiled, that was the response he wanted. "If there's a slouchy enough sweater, I can do without a bra, but I'd really prefer sweatpants or leggings."

"Hmm. I think I can accommodate that for you, but bare feet…"

She shook her head. "Once a Dom, always a Dom. I suppose I should be grateful you don't want stilettos."

"They've never done much for me. I think I see them as a potential weapon, especially for a brat like you, but I'm also always concerned the woman is going to fall off the things and break an ankle, but sweatpants are helpful to have around if you or someone else needs clothing in a hurry—they're very forgiving in size ranges. I have some in my office; come and get them."

"Why do I get the feeling that you're going to see me naked one way or another?" she asked, archly.

"Because you are as intelligent as you are sexy and beautiful."

"You're terrible."

"I am," he agreed. "Take your shower, baby. I'll be in my office."

He forced himself to walk away from her when what he really wanted was to strip her naked and sink into her wet heat. Jen was dead and there was nothing he could do for her other than to bring her killer down. If justice eluded him, he would settle for a bullet to the bastard's brain. Right now, his emotions were spinning out of control, and he needed that control back.

King was pissed that Jen was dead. He'd liked her a great deal and she'd shown some promise for turning into a field op, but he knew Samantha had spoken the truth when she told him the only one responsible was the man who had pulled the trigger. King agreed. A part of him hoped it was a simple, random act of violence, but in his heart, he knew the murder was connected to Samantha.

From the moment Samantha had made the decision to walk through the doors of Cerberus' headquarters, King knew the chances of her stalker evading justice had been slim to none. With the murder of one of his employees, it had gone to none… less than none, really. Samantha's stalker had made a bad choice when he'd chosen to threaten her and an even worse one when he'd killed one of the members of the Cerberus team. The fact that the stalker had escalated to killing had ensured that King wouldn't stop coming for him, no matter what.

King meant to make him pay for Jen's death, and to neutralize the continued threat he posed to Samantha. Neither were allowable offenses in his world.

Once inside the bullpen, he grabbed a pair of leggings from the credenza that held random clothing for field ops to use. He didn't remove any of the various tops even though some of them could be classified as a 'slouchy sweater.' His own sweater on her would qualify as slouchy and would send a not-so-subtle message to the others that Samantha Butler was off limits.

Sitting down at his desk, he drew out one of his sweaters he kept in the file drawer and placed it atop the leggings. King placed a conference call to two of his best people, Royce Sanders and Seth Newcomb. He knew Adam might take umbrage at his titular possession of the Cerberus employees, but Adam's position with Cerberus was purely administrative. All operations ran through King, and he meant to bring that power to bear on the stalker. Besides, he already had Fitz's backing and that was before the stalker had killed Jen.

"Seth? Royce? I need you both in the office. A little while ago a new client walked through the doors. She's a member of Baker Street and a well-known romance novelist. Some asshole started stalking her and she got spooked in London. I sent Jen to Union Station to pick up the bag she stashed there. Jen was shot to death in an alley close by."

"Holy shit," breathed Seth.

"Bastard. Do the cops know anything about the client?" asked Royce.

"No, and I'd prefer to keep it that way."

"Agreed," said Royce. "What do you need from us?"

"We're going to need to get up-to-snuff quickly on what's going on. We aren't fully staffed, and Adam and Chelsea are taking a little time off. I'd prefer not to interrupt that."

"Probably a good idea," said Seth. "Last time I saw Chelsea, she was a bit crispy around the edges. Adam apologized for her and said she gets that way when she needs more hands-on dominance from him."

"I got the cops to hold off on notifying her family and said we'd bring down her employee fingerprints so they can make a positive ID. Before I call her folks, I want to know at least as much as the cops know."

"Without letting them know all we know," said Royce.

"Where's the client?" asked Seth.

"She's in the security suite up here on the third floor and is aware she is here for the duration."

"Good. Then it sounds like you've got things under control until we get there."

"Why don't you shoot me a copy of Jen's finger-prints and I'll head directly to the morgue," offered Royce.

"Good id..." King ceased speaking before finishing the word.

The ability to speak was taken away when he

heard her enter his office and swiveled around to see her sashaying her way toward him without a stitch of clothing on. His imagination had not done her justice.

Samantha Butler was extraordinarily beautiful… as in drop dead, willing to kill for beautiful. Tall with a nipped in waist, an hourglass figure and a rack that was an adolescent boy's dreams. But her legs… her legs seem to go on forever and it didn't take much for him to imagine them wrapped around his waist as he plowed into her.

"King, are you there?" asked Seth.

King tried to shake his reverie. "Uh, right. Yes, I'm here. Royce, I'll send you the fingerprints. Seth, you head into the office. I deleted Jen's access codes so we should still be secure, but I'm locking down the third floor. Seth, make a thorough sweep of the lower floors before you come up."

"Got it, boss," said Seth. "I'll be with you shortly."

"I'll call in as soon as I'm through at the morgue," said Royce.

Ending the call, he couldn't stop the wolfish grin that spread across his face. "I'm not so sure I want to give you the clothes I grabbed for you. I can tell you this much, if I didn't have two other Doms headed in here, you'd stay naked. You are gorgeous. I'd better never hear you make any kind of disparaging remark about your intelligence or appearance. That'll get you spanked so hard and so fast, you won't know what happened."

"Hmmm… I think I'll take that as a compliment. Now, may I have the clothes?"

He glanced at his watch. "Not so fast. It'll take Seth at least an hour to get here and do a sweep of the office. It's going to be a long night. How about you just let me look for a few minutes."

Samantha shook her head. "You are totally obnoxious."

"True enough. But your nipples and the scent of your arousal say my kind of obnoxious turns you on." He shook his head as the chill of Jen's death settled over him. "I'm sorry. You must think I'm a callous, insensitive brute."

She rushed to his side and slid into his lap like she'd belonged there for years. "I don't. I think we're both in shock and trying to find our footing. I need you to convince me I'm not responsible for that girl's death and that you'll find whoever did this. And that has nothing to do with what hearing you tell me you think I'm beautiful did for my rather beaten-up ego and sense of self-esteem."

He pulled her closer to his body, cradling her and getting her to rest her head on his chest. "You are beautiful, and you are not responsible for what happened to Jen. And before you go there, neither am I. There was no reason to think Jen wouldn't be perfectly safe. I'm going to text Royce to get copies of the crime scene pictures. They may give us a clue as to how it happened. I'll also get our people working CCTV."

"Should we tell them about me?"

"Not until we know more. If they come across anything that leads them to you and then to us, we'll cooperate, but Jen was one of ours and we will take the lead whether CPD likes it or not."

"I'm not sure how I feel about that."

He was inclined to tell her that her feelings about it were irrelevant, even though he knew they weren't. He wanted to seize control and keep her safe, but she wasn't ready for that… not yet, anyway.

"I understand. But I ask you to at least trust me… trust Cerberus to keep you safe. You didn't go to CPD this afternoon, you came here to us."

"And maybe if I hadn't, Jen would still be alive."

That caught King up short. "I thought you agreed that you weren't responsible."

"Intellectually, I know that's true in the same way that *intellectually,* you know it's true that you aren't responsible. But can you honestly tell me that down deep in your gut you aren't wondering what if?"

She had him there. He nodded. "If you're willing to lay your cards on the table, I guess I have no choice but to do the same. Yes, I keep asking myself what if, but that doesn't do any good and helps no one, including Jen. In fact, the only one it could possibly help is the sonofabitch who killed her."

"How do you figure that?"

"If we focus on our own feelings of guilt, we'll be hunting him with one hand behind our backs."

She grinned. "I'm pretty sure you have no intention of letting me in on the hunt so no handicap on me."

"Yeah, but then I'll be all concerned that you're feeling guilty and either want to reassure you or spank the hell out of you for that."

"Would that make you feel better?"

"What?" he asked, taken by surprise.

It had been a long time since anything had taken him by surprise, but Samantha Butler seemed to excel at it.

"Spank me. It's funny, but I've always seen any sessions I get…"

"Can we not talk about other men disciplining you or what you do for them in return?"

The mischievous grin became a broad smile. "What's the matter, Coltraine, jealous?"

"Maybe. In answer to your question, yes; putting you over my lap and spanking your ass a vivid shade of red and then having you cuddle in my lap would go a long way toward making me feel a little more in control."

He held his breath while she considered his answer. "Right here? Right now? Isn't someone on their way in?"

King glanced at his watch. "Yes, but we have at least forty-five minutes."

"Why?"

"Because you asked, and because I think it would do both of us a world of good. In fact, I'll go you one better. How about we sign a D/s contract for the duration of your case? You trust me to keep you safe from the stalker, but will you also trust me to see to all of your other needs?"

"This is not what I expected."

"And yet, here you are, sitting curled up naked in my lap."

"You have a point. And yes, I do trust you to keep me safe and I think I would be a fool to turn down your offer. You need to know I'm probably going to bugger this up badly. I've never had an exclusive Dom and if I'm going to give over to you…"

He placed a finger on her lips. "Hush. I would never sign a contract with a sub with whom I didn't intend to be exclusive. Don't worry about screwing up, that's what discipline is for," he teased, and she blushed.

Samantha was fascinating. She was sitting here naked in his lap as his cock throbbed beneath her, and yet teasing her about spanking that gorgeous ass of hers made her blush. She was something of a conundrum—one he meant to figure out.

Just as quickly as she had seemed to acquiesce, her body seemed to go still. "I don't know. Maybe you should just put me back on a plane to England…"

"Why?"

"You don't know me. I don't know you."

"But you're willing to sign your first D/s contract with me."

"I didn't say that..."

"Didn't you? Look, Samantha, I don't take the lifestyle lightly. I've never signed a contract with a sub before either, so we'll both screw it up. The contract can give us a way to work it out so that we can move forward. I don't know how I'm feeling about you or why it's important to me to be your Dom, but it is. I do know that I want to keep you alive, and I want to know what it would feel like to be your Dom. Will it work for either of us long term? Who knows? But I do know something about you calls to me, and for the first time, I want to find out what that feels like, don't you?"

"And when you catch this bastard, and I have no doubt you will, what then?"

"I don't know, and neither do you. Why don't we sign a contract for the duration of your case? I know that knowing you trust me to take care of you and give over control to me will make me feel a lot more settled and I think it will do the same for you. At the end, we can look at where we are and decide whether or not we want to go on. What do you say?"

He wasn't sure what the emotion that passed across her face was—sadness, fear, doubt, longing?

"I think I say yes. I think the safest I've felt in the last several months was here with you. So, yes, Sir."

He wasn't sure what to say, but knew a kiss was far safer than trying to figure that out. He lowered his mouth and from the moment their lips touched, she yielded to his kiss as he began an exquisite exploration. He didn't know what had just happened, but he was quite sure his life would never be the same again.

CHAPTER 8

SAMANTHA

What had she just agreed to? She couldn't believe she was not only willing to sign a D/s contract, which she knew wasn't legally binding, but with a man she barely knew. What she did know was that she had spoken the truth. She'd never felt safer in her entire life than she did when she was with Coltraine or when he assured her she was safe.

"Do you really want to do this now?" she asked.

"I think we might both feel better, and I have a feeling that it's going to be a long afternoon and night. When we're done, I'm going to want you to go get some sleep."

"I'm not tired."

"First rule: you don't lie to me or any member of my team. You're exhausted. It's written all over you. Part of being your Dom is taking care of you and that means seeing that you get what you need, be it discipline, a stress release session, or sleep. Second rule: disobeying me comes with consequences."

He helped her off his lap. "I'll get the contract done tonight, but for the moment let's just operate under the general one we both have with Baker Street."

She nodded. She couldn't understand why suddenly standing in front of him, knowing he was going to spank her, she felt shy. She was a bit of an exhibitionist; he'd already seen her stark naked; and yet she felt the urge to cover herself.

"No, Samantha. Rule three: you don't get to hide yourself from me. You're so beautiful, it almost hurts my eyes to look at you."

She knew this was the point of no return—she was either in or she was out. If she was in, she would get to explore something she'd only just begun to realize she craved. If she was out, she was certain they would protect her, but she'd never know if that thing Kingston Coltraine had awakened in her would ever be fully realized with anyone else.

Samantha allowed him to guide her over his knee as he closed his other leg behind hers, trapping her so that her ass was in the highest, most vulnerable spot. His cock throbbed beneath her. At least she knew he truly desired her. There was no faking his rampaging dick. He was incredibly hard and she could feel her assessment of his equipment was not off in the slightest. If anything, she'd underestimated it.

His hand covered her ass, rubbing softly with a gentle touch. "Beautiful," he breathed. "How long have you been writing?"

She didn't want questions and answers, she wanted to get on with it, but figured confirming his assessment that she was a brat probably wasn't the way to go unless she wanted discipline from him and not just stress relief.

"Almost ten years. For the first six, I had a day job and wrote part of the time under a pen name. A lot of authors do to keep their employers from knowing. Four years ago, I won an online gaming contest. Not millions of dollars, but enough to cover all my living expenses and then some for at least two years. I gave myself that time to see what I could do if I wrote full time. So I quit my day job and did just that."

"Brave girl."

"That's not what most people thought. Most of my friends and my employer thought I was stupid."

"They were wrong."

His hand went still and she had to remind herself to breathe. She felt the brief uptake of air and waited for his hand to crack down on her ass, sending heat, pain, and arousal radiating out from where he landed the first blow.

It had been a while since she'd had any kind of session and more than a year from the last spanking.

Spankings were far more intimate than being bound to a St. Andrew's cross and flogged or feeling the sting of a whip. Normally it took a lot to get her to subspace or to cry, but here and now, she could feel the tears beginning to well on the third slap.

Samantha wondered if it was because for the first time there was meaning behind the act other than she wanted it and someone was willing to do the deed. She wondered if she'd ever felt a need reciprocal to the one coming from the man whose hand continued to smack her ass. Somewhere in the past few hours she and Coltraine had formed some kind of relationship. She wasn't sure what it was, but if felt more right than anything she'd had in a very long time.

As he continued to rain fire down on her backside, she realized she'd longed for something more than friendship from whatever man turned her ass a fiery shade of crimson. She wanted more than a competent spanking for a competent blow job—service exchanged for service. Each strike of his hand sent fire rushing through all of the synapses of her body.

"Are you all right, Samantha?"

"Yes, Sir."

The pain began to fade and become something so much more. It wasn't that she didn't feel each slap to her ass cheeks, it was that she knew what would come in the end—a sweet peace and pleasure that she'd never found anywhere else.

She could feel her body giving over, her muscles

relaxing as he spanked her. She hadn't even realized what she was missing and was still cognizant enough to know that it had never been like this with any other man. What would it feel like to truly explore the lifestyle with an experienced Dom?

This was a place where nothing from the outside could reach her—no deadlines, no story issues, no one vying for her attention. No, here all she had to do was accept his authority over her. He'd promised to see to her needs. She wondered if he meant all of them.

Samantha lost count of the number of times his hand connected with her now heated and painful flesh. It wasn't important. What was important was that he was giving her what she needed, and she felt she was doing the same for him.

The last few months had been so stressful. No, that wasn't it... they had been terrifying. The small fear growing with each escalating message from the killer. The tears flowed freely and she began to sob, not so much from the physical pain, but from the release of the tension and growing fear she'd been experiencing. All the pain and anxiety she'd been holding onto seemed to start melting away.

Finally, he didn't raise his hand to bring it back down. Instead, he let it rest lightly on her stinging backside.

"How are you, Samantha?"

"I'm fine, Sir."

"You took your spanking well."

He helped her to stand and then pulled her back into his lap, ignoring the wince she didn't manage to hide when her well-spanked ass hit his lap. For what it was worth, his cock still throbbed beneath her.

She leaned into his body, longing to be cradled against his strength again. He obliged by pulling her close. One hand trailed his fingers along the inside of her thigh. She let her legs fall open of their own accord. Her ass wasn't the only thing that was hot and in need of soothing. Her nipples were almost painful, and she was fairly certain she was dripping on his jeans.

It wasn't just his cock that was throbbing. Her entire body trembled at his touch, and she had to remind herself to breathe each time his hand came close to her pussy. Coltraine traced lazy lines along the inside of her thigh, and she thought she might scream in frustration if he didn't touch her more intimately.

Coltraine drew his finger up the inside of her leg, only this time he didn't hop to the other and trace a line down it. No, this time, he allowed his hand to cover her mound and to part her labia, exposing her pussy and her engorged clit.

"Do you know how good you feel?" he murmured almost to himself.

"Only because you made me feel that way. I have a confession to make. It's been a while since I even indulged in a session, but I haven't had a spanking in more than a year."

Samantha gasped as his finger traced circles around her clit, which was every bit as swollen and needy as his cock.

"Why does that not surprise me?" he chuckled. "Can I ask why?"

"You can ask, but I'm not sure I can tell you. Please note that isn't because I'm refusing to tell you. I just don't know that I have an answer."

"Fair enough."

His finger didn't stop swirling around her clit until he dragged it down and penetrated her core with it. She had to focus and bite her lip to keep from coming on the spot. He stroked her inner walls with a knowing touch, and as he curled his finger up inside her, he pressed down on her clit with his thumb.

"Come for me, Samantha," he ordered in a deep, dark voice that promised untold pleasure for her obedience.

Samantha's back arched and she cried out as he stroked her through the powerful orgasm that hit her with the force of a freight train. Her body trembled and her pussy convulsed as she responded uninhibitedly to his touch. When the spasms that had wracked her body were through, he continued to hold her and let her come back to herself.

"Better?" he crooned.

Unable to think, much less form words and speak, she nodded.

Coltraine stood up, lifting her as if she weighed nothing. "I was going to go tuck you in bed, but I don't want you that far from me. The couch is pretty comfortable." He walked over and deposited her there, going back to his desk and returning with his sweater. "Put this on."

"What about the leggings?"

"You won't need them," he said, opening the closet in his office and removing a pillow and what appeared to be one of the cashmere blankets Baker Street was known for. He placed the pillow at one end. "Stretch out." When she did so, she was rewarded with his covering her up. "Close your eyes and try to go to sleep. I should be either right here or just outside in the bullpen. I'll watch over you."

"Sleep isn't what I had in mind," she said demurely.

He pressed a light kiss on her mouth. "It wasn't my first choice to fulfill my own needs, but it is what you need most. Go to sleep, Samantha. Once I get Seth and Royce started, I'll need to take care of things, including notifying Jen's parents and bringing Fitzwallace up to speed. Go to sleep. You're safe."

She watched him move back to his desk, taking a seat in the chair he used to give her the spanking. She wondered if she'd ever be able to look at that chair and not think of it as the place something had started. Whether that thing lived up to its promise or not had yet to be seen.

CHAPTER 9

KING

Someday he would tell her what it had cost him to settle her on the couch in his office rather than taking her to bed and having at her the way he really wanted to. Knowing he couldn't indulge his need to fuck her long and hard, he'd opted for knowing she was close. King knew she'd be just as safe in the security suite, but the idea of her naked in a bed had been too much for his jangled nerves to tolerate.

King smiled down at her as she succumbed to being on edge for months, the ensuing exhaustion, the time differential between London and Chicago, and finally feeling safe. He was fairly sure she'd fallen asleep as soon as she closed her eyes. He indulged his need to touch her and reached down to stroke her hair. He'd never been a big fan of blondes—he wondered what the hell had been wrong with him.

Samantha was blonde and she was gorgeous or maybe it was just that she was gorgeous to him.

It didn't matter.

For him, there was a connection to her he'd never experienced before with anyone. Somewhere in the dim recesses of his mind, King knew he should be questioning the feelings that seemed to have sprung out of thin air, but he didn't. He chose to believe in what he felt. It was his truth and it was as clear to him as anything he'd ever known.

He looked up just in time to see Seth coming through the door. He was just finishing his sweep of the office and had yet to put his gun back in its holster. King put his finger to his lips to indicate silence as he moved away from Samantha—the dream, the promise of things to come—back to the reality of now: finding Jen's killer and keeping Samantha safe.

"What the fuck, King?"

King closed the door to his office behind him so as to not disturb Samantha, his sub. *His* sub… *his* woman… he liked the sound of that.

"Yeah; it's been one hell of an afternoon."

"I hate to ask this, but isn't she some kind of novelist? Any chance its some kind of publicity stunt?"

"None."

"None?" Seth questioned.

"None." King knew it in his bones to be true. "She is clearly terrified; so much so that when she thought she was being followed, she bolted to Heathrow and took the first flight out…"

"Which conveniently landed her in Chicago…"

"What do you mean by 'conveniently'?"

"Playing devil's advocate. She's a member of Baker Street so would know Cerberus is right there. Instead of going to a known quantity and people she knows, she comes to Chicago. I'm just saying it's a bit coincidental. But before we even get to that, how the hell did Jen get involved and get herself killed?"

It was as if Seth had punched him in the gut. "Entirely my fault. I took the threats seriously. In fact, I can't understand why the cops in England didn't…"

"Maybe because she never actually reported anything to the cops? Maybe she wrote them herself."

"No." King rejected the idea out of hand. "But even if it started out that way, who killed Jen and why? Are you suggesting somehow Samantha knew who Jen was, that she'd be working today, and I'd just happen to send her out?"

Seth shook his head. "Not when you put it like that."

There was no way Samantha could have faked her fear, and no way she could have plotted a way to kill Jen.

"I spoke with Fitz," said King, "and he never even considered the idea that she might be faking it. You didn't see her Seth. I doubt she's slept much since the whole thing started, certainly not since she got on an international flight and ended up here."

"Again, I'm not buying it—at least not at face value."

King shook his head. "You never believe anyone about anything. In any event, I would think Jen getting murdered would tend to shore up Samantha's assertion that she is being threatened, or do you think she hired someone to kill Jen as part of her publicity stunt?"

"Shit," said Seth, sitting down in one of the office chairs, collapsing as if he'd been an inflated balloon that had the air let out of it. "That would tend to give credence to her story. What happened?"

"I don't know all of the particulars, but Samantha believed her stalker had followed her here to America. She left her bag in Union Station before coming here. I watched her pace back and forth in front of the building for about twenty minutes before deciding to come in. Jen's been wanting to learn more about field work, and she was a good student. I thought it was a simple grab and go. I was wrong."

"Don't go there. Anyone who knows you, including Jen, knows if you'd thought there was any chance that there was any danger, you'd never have sent her."

"So my head keeps telling me."

"Listen to it. I'm sorry about coming in here and

questioning everything you've done. I was upset about Jen. I liked her. She was a good girl."

"She was indeed."

"But you aren't responsible for her death."

"Aren't I? I'm the one who sent her."

"That might be true, but there was no way to know the killer would move against her. And you're right; unless we believe Jen's death is just a random act of violence…"

"That's not what my gut tells me."

"Mine, either. So, unless we're prepared to believe this Samantha Butler person faked a bunch of emails and then hired a killer to take out someone sent to fetch her things, then not only does our client have the problem she thought she had, but the stalker has now escalated to killer."

Nodding, King said, "What worries me is what we don't know."

"How do you mean?"

"Well, he goes from sending emails and posting private social media messages to her, to breaking into her house, and then he kills someone. There's a huge gap between the first two and the last. Normally with these things there are smaller steps leading to violence—keying her car, sending flowers, questioning her at a media event, asking to meet. None of these have happened…"

"That we know of. Maybe they did and either she didn't tell you…"

"Or she didn't recognize them as part of the pattern."

Seth nodded. "Could be. We tend to forget that normal people don't look for patterns and don't catalog all kinds of small things to see if they fit."

"Are you saying we're abnormal?"

"You don't think we are? I think the whole lot of us are weird as all get out, but I also think without weirdos like us, human beings would still be sitting in trees, picking fleas off each other."

King laughed. Seth had a skewed view of the world, but he was down-to-earth and tended to be right.

"For the record," said King, "you need to keep playing devil's advocate."

Seth didn't say anything, but arched his eyebrows in an unspoken question.

"Samantha has become my sub…"

"Whoa…"

"And while the contract will say it's for the duration of this job, I intend that it be far longer term than that."

"As in permanent?"

"As in," said King nodding.

"Royce always said when you fell, you'd fall hard and fast."

"Royce said? What? Do you and Royce sit around all day talking about me?"

"Not in a bad way. Just when we got you back, you

were broken—more inside than out, and not in a psycho killer kind of way. It was as if you preferred the shadows. It's nice to see you've decided to come back into the light. I'm happy for you, King; really."

"There's just something about her. I can't explain it and if I try to, it sounds like the plot of a bad romance novel."

"No. It sounds a lot like our fearless leader. Fitz always says that from the moment he saw JJ it was all over but the shouting."

King couldn't stop the smile that spread across his face. He hoped it wouldn't be described as wistful. Wistful wasn't something he aspired to be, but the smile was there, nonetheless. "Stupid as it sounds, I only hope I'm that lucky."

"Me, too, brother; me too." There was a hint of romantic wistfulness in Seth's tone, as well. "Where do you want me to start?"

"Let's start doing the background checks on her. I need her to sign all the documentation, but she needed sleep more than anything."

"Which security suite do you have her in?"

"The bigger one, but right now she's in my office sleeping." Seth's eyebrow arched again. "Don't start. I already admitted I may have some short-sightedness where Samantha is concerned."

"On the practical side, if you're going to be here, do we need to get you some stuff from your place?"

"Might not be a bad idea. But let's hold off until

we know what's what. I think Samantha may need to have some things picked up as well."

"I assume you plan to keep her here at the club?"

"I think it's safer. I'll be curious to see if Jen's wallet was with her or if we can tell if her ID was compromised."

"I wouldn't think so as the cops called you…"

"But the killer could have looked at it as well. I want to know if it seemed undisturbed or just what's what."

"I would think Royce would be here at any time. Should I call and get him to pick up Chinese? Do we need to call Adam or wait for him to return to take the case officially?"

"No need. I spoke with Fitz. Samantha Butler is officially a client."

"Sounds good. I'll start doing the preliminary background checks."

"I already have Baker Street's records."

"Whoa. You are moving with the speed of light."

"Yes and no. We identified her with our facial recognition software. So while she was pacing back and forth, trying to decide whether or not to come in, I downloaded her file. Knowing she identifies as a submissive made it easier to know how to deal with her from the get-go."

"That will make it easier for the rest of us as well."

King laughed. "Not really. I am of the learned

opinion that the Doms at Baker Street are idiots. They think she's a SAM."

"And she isn't?"

"No, an alpha sub with brat tendencies."

Seth rolled his eyes. "In other words, she might take orders from you, but she'll be a pain-in-the-ass to the rest of us."

"I'm afraid so. I've already told her I expect her to mind the rest of the team, but honestly, I can't see that happening."

"And the day just gets better and better. How are you feeling about all of this?"

"God when did we all start talking about feelings?"

Now it was Seth's turned to laugh. "Since we all went to work for the new and improved Robert Fitzwallace. I swear the man I once thought was the toughest sonofabitch who ever lived has really mellowed since he collared and married JJ."

"And now we all want to be just like him if we can just find the right girl."

"You think you've found her, don't you?"

"Yes. I can't figure out which frightens me more—the thought of someone wanting to kill her, or my finding that elusive part of my soul."

CHAPTER 10

SAMANTHA

It was the first time in months that she felt as though she'd actually rested while she slept. She wasn't sure if it was the release of the endorphins when she'd cried, the orgasm, the spanking, or just the man himself, but Coltraine had brought her a peace she hadn't really been prepared for.

She liked it, though.

The murmurings of muffled male voices were the first sounds that penetrated the deep sleep that had been filled with all kinds of erotic, sensual images of Coltraine. Had she really agreed to sign a contract with him? She had, and somehow, the idea wasn't making her panic. In fact, it felt a lot like the cashmere blanket wrapped around her—a kind of soft, comforting hug.

Samantha sat up, swinging her legs over the edge of the couch and shaking her hair. She knew the blonde tresses were an absolute mess. She was also dressed only in his sweater and nothing else—an image she knew would present to the rest of the world as some kind of wet dream. It wasn't that she was vain, Samantha just knew that in most people's opinions she'd won the lottery in the genetics game. She understood where they were coming from, but for Samantha she'd always felt like she looked like a blonde bimbo and was most often treated like that.

After years of having fought against the stereotype and finding it insulting, she'd accepted that she couldn't change others' first impressions and so had used it to her advantage. If showing a little leg or flashing a little cleavage got her what she wanted, so be it. Her parents were responsible for her genetic make-up, and what others thought about her—unless she cared about them— was not something she bothered herself with.

The door to his office opened and Coltraine filled the doorway with his rumpled, sexy self. The man was probably the sexiest thing she'd ever seen, and he wasn't even trying. He just exuded a sexual attraction that called to her. It was as if he had sparked a flame within her she hadn't even known existed.

"Hi," she said, a little unsure of how to act. After all, the man had seen her naked, spanked her ass with an intensity she could still feel, made her climax, and then tucked her into bed.

"No one should look as beautiful as you do," he said, leaning down to kiss her.

She wasn't sure what it was about Kingston Coltraine that made her tongue-tied and her girly parts all soft and mushy… except for her nipples, which came to immediate attention.

"Um… thanks."

"For what? Stating the obvious?"

"It's nice to be told I don't look like a bedraggled mess, but also for everything before I passed out. I didn't know I was that tired. If you like…"

"This isn't *quid pro quo*, Samantha. That was your Dom giving you what you needed."

"But don't you want…"

"Of course I do. You are a gorgeous, sexy woman and I can't wait until I'm balls deep in you, but that's going to have to wait until later. Seth's here and is making the call to Jen's folks. He knew her better than I did and has actually met them before. Royce is on his way in. He's going to stop and pick up Chinese."

"I had almost forgotten about poor Jen." She sank her head into her hands, shaking it back and forth. "What does that say about me?"

It says I'm an awful, self-absorbed person that's what it says. That poor woman is dead.

"All it says is that after several months of not

sleeping well, your Dom was able to help you relax and feel safe and you got to rest. That had nothing to do with Jen. As you pointed out to me, the only person responsible for Jen's death is her murderer, who we also believe is your stalker."

"We, as in you and I."

"No, we, as in you, me, Seth, Fitz, and Royce."

"What did they have to say?"

"Seth is out in the bullpen and has swept the building to make sure we are secure. Royce went down to the morgue and had a chance to talk with the medical examiner as well as some of the detectives. They are a bit miffed that you didn't speak to them first."

"The police in London blew me off, and I had no way of knowing something would happen to Jen," she said, hotly.

"No, you didn't, but they're going to want to talk to you. We'll set it up so that we have the home court advantage."

"Can you do that here? I know that in London, Scotland Yard tends to defer to Cerberus and works with them cooperatively, but you're relatively new to America and Chicago."

"Not really. We've done enough work in this country anyway and here in Chicago that it made sense to open a branch office, so-to-speak, in the windy city. But then again, we tend to go our own way and serve our client's needs regardless of what the locals think about it. We have as many detractors as we have friends."

"You should probably give me those leggings."

"No. The first thing that's going to happen is that you're going to sign all the paperwork I need you to sign."

For the first time, she noticed he actually did have several sheets of paper in his hand. "What are all of those?"

"The first one is the contract, engaging us on your behalf. The second is a standard D/s contract that states I will be acting as your Dom for the duration of this assignment. I filled in the hard and soft limits from your general contract at Baker Street. Make sure they are still correct, that I noted them correctly and that you understand mine as well. Your contract said you were on birth control, were routinely tested, and didn't mind bareback play."

She blushed. "I like the feeling of swallowing a man's cum. I don't normally have penetrative inter-course and I know most guys prefer not to use a condom for oral sex."

"So clinical," he chuckled. "How do you feel about my fucking you without a condom? I just had my physical and am clean."

"I think I'd prefer that."

He smiled.

"What?"

"You have interesting safe words. Check for stop; draw for a break; and rook for everything is fine."

"What can I say? I love chess, and my favorite piece has always been the rook, thus why it's the name I gave my avatar. In case you missed it, I don't get out much into the real world."

"Why is that?"

"Because in the real world, I can't write the scenarios and endings the way I want them to be."

"How do you want them to be?"

"I want the good guys to win. I want there to be justice in the world and I most definitely want my happily ever after."

"Good to know. I'll see if we can't make that happen for you."

Unsure of what to say to him, in light of his earnest proclamation, she said, "If you give me a pen to sign those, I will."

He walked over to his desk, and she followed him, almost jumping out of her skin when she picked up the pen to sign and he allowed his hand to drift down and cup her ass. She became acutely aware at that moment of three things: first, the spanking he'd given her might have been for stress relief, but the sting remained; second, she found Kingston Coltraine wildly attractive; and third, she liked not only the feel of his hand resting on her bare skin, but that he hadn't felt the need to ask. She was in way over her head, but it didn't feel as if she was drowning.

"There you go," she said signing the last one with a flourish and handing him the pen. "Should we shake on it?"

"No, baby, that's not the way one concludes a D/s contract with her Dom."

He leaned down, his lips claiming hers. She was acutely aware that the walls of Coltraine's office weren't solid except for the lower half. The upper half were all glass—bulletproof glass, he had assured her. There was no hesitancy, no ask in the way his mouth covered hers. He was in control and expected her to follow, which she was all too willing to do. He pulled her close—one arm wrapped around her waist, the other pressing her lower body into direct contact with his ridiculously hard, thick, long cock.

His tongue traced the seam of her lips and they seemed to part of their own accord. He didn't need an invitation. Her acquiescence, her surrender, her submission was all he seemed to need. His tongue slipped into her mouth, gently stroking her own and encouraging hers to come and dance with his.

Samantha wondered why it was she thought she didn't like kissing? Usually, it felt awkward at best and sometimes downright icky, but this was neither. This was right and seductive and necessary. She melted against him and was rewarded by the sweetest groan as his one hand squeezed her ass.

Her hands drifted up his arms, resting on the bulging biceps she felt beneath his shirt. The man was cut. The arm that had been around her waist now stretched up as he fisted her hair, tilting her head back. He kissed along her jawline, and she could smell his delicious aroma. There was nothing fake or chemical about it. It was clean and masculine and divine.

She rubbed against his body like an alley cat in heat. She needed him in so many ways and the acknowledgment of that scared her to death. It seemed that all he had to do was get near her and her body lit up like Tower Bridge during the holidays. It wasn't flashy or explosive, just a warm energy that surged seamlessly through her system.

As he lifted his head, Samantha stood on her tiptoes and initiated another kiss. Grasping the front of his Henley, she clung to him and briefly wondered how this might work, then realized she didn't care. She vaguely remembered someone else was in his office, but she knew if he threw her down and covered her body with his, she wouldn't do anything to stop him. In fact, she'd spread her legs and invite him to make a home for himself there.

Falling for Kingston Coltraine was a dangerous proposition. She knew who he was and what he'd done. She'd heard the whispers at Baker Street. The kindest descriptors of his emotional availability were distant and contained. Most just said he was cold and dead inside and had nothing of emotional substance to offer a woman. The last thing she needed was to fall head over heels for some guy who only wanted one thing from her. The same thing that so many men had wanted in the past: a nice piece of arm candy that they could fuck whenever they wanted.

It was the reason Samantha had withdrawn into her career as a romance novelist. If she couldn't find what she wanted in the real world, she would write how she wanted it to be for others. Between writing and her active online gaming life, she was happy—or at least as happy as she'd been before. It had taken time and determination to get what and where she wanted, and she had no intention of letting anyone derail her plans.

Until now, holding to that goal had never been in danger. But with Kingston Coltraine seeming to dangle every dream, romantic notion and happily ever after she'd ever entertained, she was concerned that her plan to hold to her ever continuing success was in danger of going up in smoke.

Coltraine's finger now trailed up the crack of her ass, tapping against her tight little rosebud and making her squirm. She'd never had any desire to experience anal intercourse… until now. She'd have to add it to her soft limits. Samantha had a sneaky suspicion those soft limits would be pushed.

"King," said a voice from the door. "Sorry; I didn't see you."

"The hell you didn't. Two of the walls of this office are glass." He opened his eyes and looked down into hers. There was a lazy flame of desire flickering there. This was a man who knew he had the woman in his arms right where he wanted her—aroused and unwilling to deny him anything. "What the fuck do you want?"

"I just spoke to Royce. He's on his way in. He's got the unofficial police file and is going to stop and get Peking duck, orange chicken, Mongolian beef, fried rice, and eggrolls. He wants to know if you or the client want anything else."

Coltraine looked down at her, quirking his eyebrow. She grinned. "Do they make pan-fried dumplings?"

He chuckled. "They do, indeed. Seth, ask Royce to bring Samantha some dumplings."

"Hey Samantha, I'm Seth."

"Hi, Seth."

"Get out, Seth," growled Coltraine.

"Okay for now, but eventually you're going to have to let her get dressed…"

"Not necessarily," Coltraine drawled, and Samantha felt a blush crawling up her face. "You can write romance novels in the nude, can't you, baby?"

Samantha smiled sweetly. Coltraine was about to find out she wasn't the meek, mild sub he considered her to be. "Of course. I can also bring my knee up into your ball sac in the nude."

Instead of his smiling eyes going dark or even narrow, they danced with merriment as his friend Seth guffawed loudly as he said, "Oh, I like her. Fair warning, Samantha, he can be a bit of a bastard when he tries and takes this whole D/s thing fairly seriously."

Samantha wrapped her arms around his neck. "Is he right? Do you take this whole lifestyle thing seriously?"

"I already told you that, but more than that, you'll be the first sub to ever wear my collar."

"What if I don't want to wear your collar?" she teased.

"As I said, the dungeon is fully functional. I can make you beg to take my collar."

"Don't let him threaten you like that, Samantha. I have so much more to offer than he does as a Dom."

"The fuck you... ouch, shit, Samantha," Coltraine sputtered as she kicked him in the shin.

"Oh, please, my bare foot on your muscled leg over a pair of jeans? Besides, I'm entitled."

"How do you figure that?"

"You're snarling at your friend over what? Me? As in you think I'd take him up on his less-than-sincere offer?"

"Careful, King, that's a trick question. If you say yes, she kicks you again for being a jealous asshole and if you say no, she kicks you again for not trusting her."

"I'll just follow Fitz's example," King said as his mouth swooped down to capture hers in a kiss that was devastating in its ability to render her breathless.

As he relinquished her lips, he said "I'm sorry. Lesson learned."

She snuggled against him, happier than she could remember being in a long time and knowing that it made absolutely no sense at all. Wasn't that what life was about—risking it all without being certain of the outcome?

CHAPTER 11

SAMANTHA

a buzzer sounded, startling her, but when she tried to move away, Coltraine held her steady.

"Royce is here. Shall we eat in the war room?" asked Seth, who seemed to be ignoring the fact that she was dressed in Coltraine's sweater.

"Probably the most comfortable," said Coltraine with a nod.

"War room? Wouldn't this floor be more secure?" asked Samantha.

"We have two conference rooms. The one on the second floor where we met earlier and a smaller, more secure one on this floor that we affectionately refer to as the war room. We generally don't let clients up on this floor at all and never in that room. We keep a lot of secure information and plans here. But I want to start building our case and we have white boards and all kinds of electronic shit in there."

"War room it is," said Seth, leaving them alone.

"Can I have the leggings?" she asked.

"No. But I'll give you a choice. You can either join Royce, Seth, and I in the conference room and be included in the discussion, or you and I can have dinner in the suite and when we're done, I'll tuck you in bed and then go spend time with Seth and Royce so that all three of us are up to speed."

"I thought… I mean, I got the impression… Never mind. I guess I thought you wanted more from me. Go eat with your friends. I'll be fine in the suite."

She turned to leave but was prevented when he grabbed her arm. "Let me be crystal clear. I want nothing more in this life than to sink balls deep in you and hear you screaming my name. If you choose to have dinner with Royce, Seth and me, you will have on nothing more than my sweater, will eat sitting in my lap and will hopefully leave a wet spot on my jeans."

Samantha could feel heat and color creeping up her face. The heroes she wrote often spoke this boldly and plainly to the women in their lives, but never once had any man told her quite so directly what he wanted and expected. Kingston Coltraine scared the hell out of her, but she was also drawn to him in an inexplicable way she couldn't seem to resist. The real issue, of course, was that she wasn't sure she wanted to.

"In that case, I choose having dinner with the three of you."

He grinned at her. "Good answer."

He grasped her hand and led her into the conference room next to Adam's office from which the aroma of Chinese food wafted out to greet her. When she'd first met Coltraine, she'd thought he looked more like a male model than the head of ops for Cerberus in America. Then she'd met Seth and found it difficult to believe that he was some kind of lethal weapon, as all of the field people in Cerberus seemed to have been picked more for their good looks than their deadly skills. And now she was meeting Royce, who was every bit as disarmingly gorgeous as he was supposed to be deadly.

"Ms. Butler," he said walking toward her and extending his hand, "I'm Royce Sanders. I believe you ordered pan-fried dumplings. Good choice. They are excellent. I see you have on King's sweater, but no collar, which means there is still hope."

"Only if you want me to break your damn nose," said Coltraine as he sat down in one of the chairs, pulling Samantha into his lap. "We've been working on a fast track here. She'll be wearing a collar before the club officially opens."

Royce grinned and looked at Seth. "You're right, he is a bit possessive."

"Don't listen to them, Samantha. They're just giving me shit. Seth, you talked to Jen's parents?" Coltraine asked, taking a plate and heaping it high with the various choices. He selected only one set of chopsticks and then deftly picked up one of the pan-fried dumplings and offered her the first bite. She'd written about this kind of thing in her books but had never been in the position of sitting half-naked in some guy's lap as he offered to feed her.

"They were, understandably, shocked and upset. I assured them we would find whoever was responsible and make him or her pay…" started Seth.

"It has to be a man, doesn't it?" asked Samantha. "I mean most stalkers are men…"

"Yes, but we don't like to exclude anyone when we're first starting," explained Coltraine.

"But she's right; more than eighty-five percent of stalkers are male. But as King says, we're too early in the game…" said Royce.

"It's not a game to me," said Samantha, "and I doubt Jen's parents would see it that way either."

"I stand corrected, and that was a bad word choice on my part."

"As I was saying," said Seth, "they are grateful we are taking the lead. I told them we'd put pressure on the medical examiner's office to try and get her body released for burial. I told them we'd handle the transport back to Omaha personally. I also gave them our deepest condolences. Her father was a wreck, but her mom said Jen had loved working for Cerberus and had spoken highly of everyone here."

"Good," said Coltraine with a nod. "I keep coming back to, why kill her?"

"What do you mean?" asked Royce.

"She wasn't dressed like Samantha; but Jen and Samantha were of similar height and build. Samantha is a bit more top heavy, but Jen had planned to wear clothes that concealed her shape. Jen was going to get Samantha's things and stick them in a bag she brought with her. So what made the guy go after Jen?"

"Maybe he spotted her coming out," said Seth.

"No," said Coltraine. "Jen wasn't going to use Samantha's bag. Jen was going to put Samantha's things in her bag and leave Samantha's duffel in the locker. The only way the killer could have linked Jen to Samantha was if he saw Jen moving the clothes over and wanted to send a signal that he was watching."

"You don't think the killer mistook Jen for me?"

"I wouldn't think so, but if he's escalating maybe he wasn't paying attention to their differences. They were about the same height, but their builds are different. Samantha has far more curves…"

"Writing can be stressful so sometimes I reach for the M & M's…"

"There's nothing wrong with curves, Samantha. I have no idea why it is that women try to starve themselves until you can count their ribs and stab yourself on their hip bones. You and Jen may have been of similar height, but you are way more curvy. There's no way anyone could mistake you two for each other, even at a distance… and wasn't Jen shot close up?"

Royce nodded. "As far as the medical examiner can tell, the killer held Jen around the neck while he shot her point blank twice. The body didn't seem to be searched or positioned or anything like that. Just shot and killed and placed on her back, staring straight up."

"That's pretty bold—two shots in broad daylight? Even in the rain and with a silencer…" said Seth.

"Yes, but in an alley, so some attempt to be unseen."

"I think it goes along with the escalation," said Royce. "By the way, the cops want to talk to Samantha. I told them we could arrange for two of them to come here. They wanted to get pissy and have her come there, but I told them we, and she, were under no obligation. When they threatened to get a material witness warrant, I told them we'd have her untouchable before they could serve it."

"Do you think I should have gone to them? The cops in England were not only dismissive but bordered on rude. They all but accused me of making it up as a publicity stunt."

"People have done more to get their fifteen minutes of fame."

"You don't think…" Samantha started, feeling very unsure of herself.

"Full disclosure," said Seth, "I did until I saw you with King. If he trusts you, that's good enough for me."

"Same," said Royce. "On the other hand, the cops haven't seen you all cuddled up with the big bad Dom there, so…"

"Nor will they," said Coltraine. "If you want to talk to them, we'll arrange for them to come here. If not, they can go fuck themselves and if they try to pull that material witness shit, we'll show them just how much pull we have with the higher-ups in this city. I take it we're all in agreement that whoever killed Jen is most likely the same asshat stalking Samantha and that he's escalating?"

Both Royce and Seth nodded.

"I've been looking at these private messages and emails. The messages were far less aggressive and all of the profiles they were supposed to be from were either closed down or the person sending them used a completely fake profile. Royce, did they give you the tapes for CCTV?"

"No, but Sully said he could get them for us pretty quickly. We should have everything by morning—London, Heathrow, O'Hare, the Club, and the alley. We'll find the bastard," Royce assured him. "Sully is also working on trying to track back the emails. So far, he's found invented names, and they either used public servers or they bounced them all around the world, and he's having trouble finding their origin point. He's got Nina working on it, as well."

"What about the photos of the crime scene?" asked Coltraine.

"Not much there. The ME did identify that the gun used most likely was a Ruger 9MM with a suppressor." said Royce.

"Aren't they called silencers?" asked Samantha.

"Only in books, television, and movies. They don't actually silence the sound, but they do suppress it," said Coltraine.

"But how could he follow me with a gun? There's no way he could have brought that on a plane."

"Guns are easy to get, but not so easy to transport. One of the ways professionals do it is transport their silencer disguised as something innocuous in a carry-on or just wrapped up to disguise the shape in a checked bag. Then they buy a cheap gun on the streets wherever they're going and they're good to go."

"Even if they find a gun," said Seth, "which I doubt they will, there won't be any way to trace it back to whoever killed Jen. Whoever did this didn't go into a gun store and make a legal sale. They bought a street gun. It could even have been used in other crimes."

"So even knowing what gun they used doesn't help us," Samantha said, quietly.

"Not a whole lot, I'm afraid. We'll let the cops run with that. That'll give them something to do and keep them out of our hair. We're going to focus on the CCTV as well as the messages and emails."

"You can rest easy. It was always a toss-up as to who was better when Nina wasn't with us. Now she is and seriously no one in the world can beat the two of them. Nobody," assured Seth.

"I suggest we settle in for the night," said Royce as he started to clean up the food. "I would suggest we lock Samantha in the suite with one of us just inside the door and rotate guards." Coltraine growled. "Yeah, I didn't think that was going to work. So how about if King provides close cover all night, and Seth and I will trade out who sits outside the door and who does roving patrols."

"That's a much better plan," said Coltraine amiably.

"Somehow, I thought that was going to be the plan."

Coltraine helped her off his lap. Samantha was embarrassed to see he'd gotten his wish. There was a telltale wet spot on his jeans where she'd been sitting. He pulled her to him and kissed her lightly but with promised passion.

"Why don't you go down to the suite and get comfortable. I won't be but a minute."

"If you're going to talk about the case, you said I would be involved."

"You will be right up to the point I say it's too dangerous and sideline you. This is not that, but I need to speak to these two knuckleheads before I join you."

He stood looking down at her, and Samantha could almost hear him ticking off the ways in which she was racking up demerits that might make the spanking he'd given her earlier pale in comparison.

"Now, Samantha," he said in what she was fast beginning to think of as his Dom voice.

She left them and headed for the big suite, wondering what the hell she was doing. A few months ago, she'd been happily finishing up her latest novel and enjoying her life. Now she was in a strange city with a man she barely knew. True, she knew the organization he worked for, but she'd never slept with a man she barely knew. The worst part was that she wasn't even worried. That wasn't true. Until he'd made it all too clear to his friends that he would be sharing a bed with her, she'd been worried he might not. Worried that he'd only wanted to spank her, although she knew from his reputation that was something he avoided. He far preferred whips and floggers to the intimacy of warming up a woman's backside with his hand.

Samantha might be a romance novelist, but in some ways, she wasn't a romantic. She didn't really believe in true love or fated mates, but meeting Kingston Coltraine had changed everything. Everything. She knew in her soul nothing would ever be the same again. In some ways that scared her as much—if not more—than whoever it was that was stalking her.

CHAPTER 12

SAMANTHA

Samantha tried to tell herself this was a mistake, but she knew it wasn't. She knew that she was in the right place with the right man. For as long as it lasted, she was going to submit to Kingston Coltraine, not just because he made her feel safe, but because she reveled in how he made her feel.

At first, sitting in his lap had made her feel awkward, but neither Coltraine nor the other two men had seemed to notice. Coltraine had held her and fed her Chinese food with chopsticks. If they were together long enough, maybe she could get him to teach her how to use them. And she wasn't positive, but she was almost sure Seth and Royce had seen the wet spot on his jeans and been envious.

Coltraine wasn't the only one who avoided intimacy in the dungeon. Samantha kept her impact play fairly impersonal—preferring to be restrained on a spanking horse or a St. Andrew's cross and having the man giving her a session use a whip or a flogger, depending on what she needed. It felt more like a service for service transaction that way. But lying over a man's lap, accepting his authority and feeling his hand as it connected with her backside was something altogether different. There had been nothing transactional or business-like in the way Coltraine had spanked her or when he'd told her he wanted to fuck her hard and long and planned to do so.

Samantha paced around the room, not quite sure what to do with herself. Should she try to arrange herself artfully in bed? No, that seemed a little too cliché. Should she get comfy in the recliner? No, too awkward to get up. Sit on the bed like an errant school girl? No, she wasn't being disciplined. What the fuck was she supposed to do?

You're a submissive in a BDSM club, dummy. Get naked and present yourself to your Dom.

Most times the little voice inside her head told her to do really stupid things, but this time it made a lot of sense. She pulled Coltraine's sweater over her head, folded it neatly and put it on the dresser.

Even though she'd only been wearing his sweater, she'd either been tucked under the cashmere blanket or cuddled on Coltraine's lap. It was a toss-up as to which had kept her warmer. But now she had neither and the air was chillier than she'd expected it to be.

She wanted this. She wanted him. In a world that

had gone topsy-turvy on her, she wanted to have sex with Kingston Coltraine. She wanted to know what it felt like to be his sub for however long it took them to find her stalker. She wanted to feel safer than she had in months.

Samantha sank to her knees, spreading her knees wide, placing her hands palms up on her thighs and lowered her head. When Samantha had first been learning protocol, she'd found this presentation humiliating and then silly. After all, they were all adults, right? But she'd come to understand, respect, and even like it. It was a way for both parties to slip into their roles and let their cares fade away.

The door opened and then two boots came into view. "That's very nice. One thing about Baker Street that we mean to capture here at Club Southside is to train our Doms and subs. I can tell you as a Dom, there is something about a sub kneeling to serve you that just sets the right mood."

He fisted her hair, tugging her head back. "Look at me Samantha." She did so. "I know I pushed you into signing that contract, but you don't have to do this…"

"You don't want me?" she asked, tenuously.

"You're kidding, right? I'm a guy. From the moment I saw you standing in the foyer, I wanted you. I'm a Dom. From the second you trusted me to give you what you needed in terms of a spanking, I wanted you. And now, I walk in to find the most beautiful sub

I've ever seen kneeling and naked, presenting herself to me. And you think I don't want you? Baby, if we go forward, you might not be able to walk tomorrow morning."

She grinned up at him. Coltraine had a way of saying things that not only turned her on, but touched some deep place in her soul she thought would never see the light of day.

"If you tell me rook, then we're on and you're going to get what I promised you. I'll have you collared before noon tomorrow. I'll fuck you so many times tonight, that you'll forget what it's like not to have my cock shoved deep in your pussy. I'll fuck you anywhere, anyway, and anytime I like. I won't always ask either, sometimes I'll just put you in whatever position I want and have at you. You get bratty with me and I'll spank your ass silly before I put you on your belly and fuck you from behind."

She trembled, not from fear but from desire. Each line he'd spoken had set off endorphins in her system. Her nipples were hard, not because of the cool air, but because she wanted him so badly.

"Where are you, Samantha?"

Did he think she was so horny she'd forgotten where they were? She looked into his eyes and smiled. He wasn't asking to see if she knew where they were. He wanted to know if she was agreeing, if she was ready.

"I'm rook, Sir. I don't know that I've ever been so rook before."

He chuckled again, the sound felt like a warm cascade of water swirling all around her and sensitizing her skin. She tore her eyes away from his and was confronted by the bulging fly of his jeans.

"You see something you want, baby?"

"Yes, Sir."

"Why don't you open my fly and let my cock come out to play. It's been hard for you all day."

"Not all day, Sir. I didn't get here until lunchtime."

"You looking to get a discipline spanking, brat?" he growled.

If the chuckle felt like a warm hug, the growl did something to awaken every sexual synapse in her body. Her nipples tightened appreciatively, and she was pretty sure she'd never been wetter in her life. Her whole sex was throbbing in anticipation, and she shivered.

"No, Sir," she said as she reached up and began unbuttoning his fly.

How many times had she written this scene? She was certain that this time, reality would be so much better than fantasy. The minute his fly was open, Coltraine's cock came out to play. It was enormous —thick, long and ready to go. The thing defied gravity as its plum-shaped head dripped a bit of pre-cum.

"Not one drop lands anywhere but your mouth or your pussy," he commanded.

She licked the pre-cum from his dick and then began to lick his length, laving her tongue down his shaft to its root and then back up again, before sucking the head inside her mouth. Bringing one hand up to cup his tight and heavy balls, she used the other to squeeze his dick as she began to suck in earnest, her tongue swirling around its head. He groaned as he placed his hand on the back of her head, pushing her down to swallow him.

"All of it, baby."

Samantha relaxed her jaw and took him all the way to the back of her throat before he drew back and began to fuck her mouth, taking away any and all semblance of control she thought she might have had.

Then he stopped. "Enough, Samantha."

He pulled on her hair with one hand and helped her to stand with the other. Swinging her up in his arms, he carried her to the bed, laying her down in the middle before sitting on the edge, removing all of his clothes, and tossing them aside.

His clothing had concealed far more than she thought. The man was nothing but slab after slab of muscle. Broad shoulders, cut chest, trim waist and thighs like tree trunks. But none of it compared to the hard cock that almost reached his navel and seemed to throb with a life of its own.

Coltraine climbed on the bed and covered her

body with his own, forcing her down into the soft mattress. He insinuated himself between her thighs, settling there and making a place for himself. His cock pressed against the opening of her pussy, hesitating for just a moment before he pressed himself inside.

Samantha moaned as he pushed into her core. She'd never been with a man anywhere close to his size. He used short, even, slow strokes to open her up. The initial discomfort gave way to pleasure as it began surging through her system, making it easier and easier for her body to accept his.

"God, yes," he murmured, resting his forehead against hers as he pressed deeper and deeper.

The thrusts became longer and more forceful, each one taking him deeper inside. His hand went under her ass to hold her steady as he began to pound into her. He kissed her, distracting her from any residual pain as he drew back and slammed into her again and again. Samantha drew her legs up, wrapping them around him as he surged forward and back and then forward again.

As he buried himself up to his root, he ground his pelvis against hers, rubbing her clit so that the orgasm she felt building was swift and strong and over-whelmed her with its power. He changed up the rhythm, hitting her G-spot and sending her flying as she cried out his name.

Over and over, he thrust into her, not letting up when she came, but just fucking her through it. He drove her toward another climax, relentlessly hammering her pussy and sending her into some rarefied space where nothing but this man existed. As she came a second time, he gave a final, brutal thrust and spilled himself in her—the warmth soothing her battered inner walls.

He collapsed on top of her, his head resting on the pillow beside her, his cock still buried deep in her core, but it was more than his cock that connected them. It was something more profound than that. She could barely breathe, not so much from the physical exertion, but from understanding that this was so much more than being fucked by him. This was the beginning of something so amazing, so enormous that all she could do was cling to him and hope it would never end.

"I won't let you go Samantha. I won't let anyone hurt you. I'll catch this bastard and make him pay for what he did to Jen and what he wanted to do to you."

It was the kind of thing she wrote for the heroes in her book to say, but she'd never believed she'd be the recipient of that kind of declaration. Maybe it was just his way of dealing with post-coital emotions, but she didn't believe that. She believed he meant it, and even if he didn't for now… she would believe.

CHAPTER 13

KING

It wasn't so much the sound of the water running in the shower that disturbed his sleep as it was the loss of her warmth beside him. King hadn't had a lot of warmth in his life. Sometime during the night, he had concluded that Samantha could bring both warmth and light to his life. Her heart and soul were buoyant, and she radiated joy, passion, and the tomorrow he hadn't realized he'd been searching for.

And that was it. Samantha represented a belief that tomorrow would always come, and with it endless possibilities for happiness.

Next, I'll be believing in rainbows and unicorns. He snorted.

The loss of her warm body curled up against his may have broken his reverie, but it was the sound of the shower running in the attached bath that brought him to full wakefulness. He glanced at his cell phone. They had time for a little one-on-one session in the shower. King left the bed but slowed as he opened the door that had been left slightly ajar.

As he entered the bath, he realized the sound of the water was covering Samantha's quiet weeping. Did she regret last night? She certainly hadn't seemed to, basking in the mutual sensuality and pleasure they had found with one another.

Samantha was standing under the water as steam filled the shower, her face buried in a washcloth as she tried to muffle the sound. She didn't want to disturb him… didn't want to burden him with her fears. He'd thought they'd made it through that, but apparently not. It was time the Dom stepped up and provided whatever it was his sub needed.

He opened the door and she whirled to face him, her blond hair falling in bedraggled locks all around her. Her eyes were swollen and red and her beautiful porcelain skin was blotchy. It was one more discovery about his woman—she was not a pretty crier.

King reached for her and felt her stiffen. That was another thing he'd thought they'd worked through. "No. You do not resist me, especially when I'm trying to comfort you." He pulled her close.

"I'm sorry," she said, trying to stifle her tears.

He brought his hand down sharply on her soft, wet backside, making her yelp and jump closer to him.

"Don't tell me what you think I want to hear. Tell me what it is you're feeling. What has you so upset?"

She shook her head and King reached past her to turn off the shower. He led her out wrapping a towel around her and rubbing her dry.

"You're going to tell me what's wrong. I can't protect you or fix whatever it is unless I know. The only way for me to know is for you to tell me. Was it last night? Did I push you too far?"

"No. god no. Last night was the best night of my life that I can ever remember. I have a bad habit of getting into my own head and staying there. It's my own little writer's retreat."

He chuckled. "Then why are you standing in the shower crying?"

"I didn't want to bother you."

"Samantha, you standing in the shower crying by yourself bothers me. Whatever is wrong we can fix. Unless someone died, we can fix it."

She looked up at him, tears beginning to well in her eyes. *Shit! Someone had died and she felt responsible. Time to clear that up right now.*

"Jen is dead," she whispered. "If I hadn't come here…"

"Her murderer would have probably killed you and Jen could have been hit by a bus tomorrow. None of us are promised tomorrow. You are no more responsible for her death than I am. If anyone other than the killer is responsible, it would be me. Do you think I'm responsible?"

"No, of course not. There shouldn't have been anything to worry about. She'd been trained. You assessed the situation and made a decision."

"Right," said King with a nod. "So, if I'm not responsible, how on earth could you be?"

Samantha banged her head lightly on his chest. "I know that whoever this asshole is, he's responsible, but…" she said, angrily.

"But nothing. I was waiting for you to get angry. Whoever he is, and we're still not ruling out a woman, has had you scared for months. Being scared puts you in a defensive position. Being angry puts you in a more assertive frame of mind. Don't get me wrong, you will stay where I can keep you safe, but at least you won't have fear as a constant companion weighing you down."

She shook her head. "I'm not normally a crying, bratty, can't control her emotions kind of girl…"

"Being stalked with no one believing you has done a number on you. Give yourself a break. By the way, at some point Fitzwallace is going to figure out that you could have gone to the team in London long before now. You might want to think about hiding behind me when that happens."

"Why would I do that?" she asked.

"Because Fitz has his thing about the people he

cares about and he cares about the people at Cerberus and at the club."

"Why would I take refuge behind you?"

"Because by then I'll have a collar wrapped around your neck and that's something Fitz will respect."

"Do you think we'll have to go back to London to catch this guy?" she asked, trying hard to keep her hand from trembling.

"Probably not."

"Then why would I be wearing your collar?"

"Because until I hear 'check' and you hand it back to me, you're my sub."

"Only until the end of the case…"

"I don't recall putting an end date in the contract," he said leaning against the vanity.

"Because you didn't know how long it would take. You had to have had some kind of end date in mind."

"Did I? You know, for a romance writer, you're not a big believer in happily ever after."

"You didn't put that down, did you? I mean I know you said you take the lifestyle seriously, but you do know D/s contracts aren't legally binding. I can terminate it at any time…"

"And my first call will be to Fitz."

"So what?"

"Baby, we run black ops all the time. Picking you up and spiriting you off to a true safe house wouldn't be much of a problem."

"You wouldn't. That's blackmail."

"I like to think of it as a persuasive argument. Listen, Samantha, you can't deny that there's something special between us, and even if you do, we'll both know you're lying. Even if you don't want to trust that, trust me to keep you safe. Trust me to be your Dom."

"Why?"

"Because I do believe in happily ever after, and I do believe we have something special. All the contract does is allow both of us to know what we expect of ourselves and each other. It really doesn't have to be any more complicated than that. If you don't want it to be anything more than a way to keep the Scotsman at bay, fine. But maybe you'll realize there's more to D/s than just a service agreement. What do you think?"

"I think you might be as crazy as my stalker, but I also think I like your crazy a whole lot better."

King came away from the vanity, cupping the nape of her neck and drawing her to him. He lowered his head to hers and gently fused their lips together. Arousal flared and then spread warmth throughout his system. Samantha was a curious creature. A part of her wanted to believe and wanted to give over, but somewhere along the line, she'd learned that the way to keep her heart safe was to stay aloof. He had no intention of allowing that.

She might think she was going to use him for sex

and to explore D/s in more depth, but King's long-term plan was for Samantha Butler to spend the rest of her life with him. He not only wanted a collar around her neck; he wanted a ring around her finger. She sagged against him, moaning as she did so, and sliding her tongue along his as he explored her mouth. Her nipples tightened and she moved into his body so there was nothing between them… not even a sigh.

He kissed her for the longest time, content just to explore her mouth, face, jaw, and neck—never moving below the hollow of her throat. As his lips moved down from her lips, he sank his fingers into her hair and tugged her head back, exposing her throat. She moaned as he trailed kisses down and back up before settling on her mouth again.

There was a knock on the door to the hallway before it cracked open.

"Go away," snarled King.

"No, can do, buddy," said Seth. "The cops called Royce. They want to talk to our client. They wanted us to bring her downtown—do you believe the jackass actually told me to 'bring her downtown.' Like what's that supposed to mean? There is more than one precinct 'downtown.'"

King kissed her lightly one more time, wrapped a towel around his waist and handed Samantha a big, fluffy bathrobe before stepping out into the main room of the suite.

"Sorry to interrupt," apologized Seth with a grin

that said he really wasn't. "Good morning, Samantha. You two had better get dressed; they should be here any time. Royce is downstairs bitching about not having adequate provisions. He's an excellent cook— probably making omelets of some kind. They're always delicious."

"I don't generally eat breakfast. Please tell Royce to not go to any trouble for me," said Samantha.

"Tell Royce Samantha said thank you for thinking of her. We'll eat in the war room."

"You might want to hurry. You know how pissy Royce can get if his food is allowed to get cold. Besides, we have some new information."

"You heard the man. We'll try and see if we can't get the contents of your bag back today, but you might want to start making a list of things you want to wear and the sizes you need."

"I thought as my Dom you dictated those kinds of things," Samantha teased.

King took a deep breath and exhaled slowly. *Brat.* "That's fine, baby, but you seemed to not like the idea of your entire wardrobe consisting of corsets, thongs, and nothing at all."

Watching Samantha blush was becoming a favorite past-time of his. She went and found his sweater and a pair of sweatpants, which were not only offensive on her beautiful body, but they were also in danger of falling off.

He pulled on his Levi's, boots and the sweater he'd

had on the night before. He would send Seth to pick her up a few things and to swing by his loft, as well, so he'd have what he needed. Until they caught the killer who was also stalking his woman, he wasn't going anywhere.

They joined Seth in the war room just as Royce carried in a big tray that had the most delicious aromas emanating from it.

"I didn't have a lot to go on. If we're all staying here, we're going to need a major food delivery. I made a hash with the leftover pulled pork, roasted potatoes, peppers, and onions. There's also mixed berries, and I toasted some rolls and there's several different types of jam."

"I said I wasn't big on breakfast, but this smells way too good not to indulge. Thank you," said Samantha.

King helped her with a plate and got her coffee before serving himself and sitting beside her. "So, what did you find?" he asked the room in general.

"The good news is Nina and Sully were finally able to get the IP address for the emails to stop pinging around the world. All of the origin locations were in London," answered Seth.

"There was more than one location?" asked King as he took a bite of the hash. "Damn, Royce, that's good."

"Thanks," said Royce with a smile.

"Yes, multiple locations. The bad news is it led

them to multiple public networks—museums, libraries, et cetera. So, then they started combing all of the CCTV tapes and kept locating what appears to be the same person. He's smart enough not to reveal his face, but his shape and size suggest he's a man."

"That's good, right?" asked Samantha.

"Yes, but without a face to use for identification, it becomes more difficult. Nina and Sully then started running what they had against tapes for both Heathrow and O'Hare…"

"None of this is legal is it?" asked Samantha in a tone that said she knew the answer and really didn't mind.

"Not in the least, which means Sully is a bit concerned and Nina is having a ball. Nina just loves to play black hat hacker."

"He followed her to O'Hare, didn't he?" asked King.

Seth nodded. "I'm afraid so. Nina found evidence of someone hacking the airlines to find your flight and destination."

"How could he do that?"

"You used your legal name, and you don't write under a pen name any longer."

"Shit. I'm an idiot."

"No, baby, you aren't. You didn't have time to get the proper fake ID—something Fitz will be sure to point out to you that had you come to them, none of it would have been necessary and that if you needed to leave the country, Nina could have set you up. We probably should ask Nina to get her a set of papers anyway."

"She's already working on it. We're trying to narrow down the list of names that might be his, but he may well have traveled under an alias."

"Anything to link him to Jen's death?" asked King.

"Not so far, but we're working on that too," answered Seth.

The buzzer from the street below rang, and they pulled up the video feed. "ID's please," said Royce over the speaker.

"Knock it off, Sanders. You know it's us."

Royce chuckled and stood. "I'll go let them in, but I am going to make them show me ID and relinquish any weapons they may be carrying."

"Returning the favor?" asked King.

"Yes. These two chuckleheads are real assholes, and for the record, they'd have blown Samantha off like their counterparts in London if she'd gone to them."

Royce left the room and King turned to her. "Let me do the talking. I don't care what they say or what questions they ask, you defer to me unless I tell you otherwise."

"Aren't they supposed to be on our side?" she asked.

"The operative phrase, baby, is 'supposed to be.'"

They watched on the screen as Royce admitted

them into the building's foyer and then had them remove their IDs so he could inspect them before taking their weapons and depositing them in the safe they kept behind the reception desk for just that purpose. When there seemed to be some resistance to the cops handing over their weapons, Royce stood silently—his arms crossed over his chest—a clear indication that it was his way or no way at all without a warrant. Once the detectives complied, Royce led them up the staircase to the second floor.

King reached up and stroked her hair. "Relax, Samantha. They may not exactly be our partners in this, but I don't think the Chicago PD is responsible for your stalker or Jen's death. We're going to meet them in the conference room on the second floor."

He stood and helped her from her seat. She took his proffered hand, and they entered the vintage elevator and took it down to the second floor. The door opened and the three of them joined Royce and the two police officers.

"Good morning, gentlemen," said King. "I understand you'd like to speak with our client."

"Yes, without your interference and downtown."

King recognized the speaker—a detective named Moore. He tried to think of anything good he'd heard about him and failed. He smiled.

"What's the old saying? People in hell want ice water, but that don't mean they get it."

"You're interfering in a murder investigation. We

believe Ms. Butler—if that's even her real name—has information that could be vital to our case. We could get a material witness warrant."

"I doubt it. If you haven't even confirmed her identity, I have very little faith in your ability to keep our client safe. If you want to try a friendly judge for a warrant, go ahead. We'll have her out of the country before the ink is dry."

The younger cop, a man by the name of Dillon, spread his hands open. "Settle down, Coltraine. Moore tends to get pissy with private security." He turned to Moore. "For the record, he's not joking. Even if we could get a warrant, we'd never be able to serve it." Dillon turned back to King. "And I don't want to get into an adversarial turf war with Cerberus. If you'd allow us access to your client, on your terms, we'd appreciate it. I'm sure you'd like to see your employee's killer brought to justice."

"We would. Now, what is it you gentlemen would like to know?"

With tempers cooled, everyone took a seat. Samantha chose to sit in the chair next to King's and scooted it closer to him. He sent her a reassuring smile, and then they began.

I may have to deal with a couple of meathead cops, but Samantha seems to be settling in. All in all, not a bad way to start the day.

CHAPTER 14

SAMANTHA

There was a part of Samantha that resented Coltraine taking the lead and answering most of the questions the detectives had. Granted, he did seem to know more about what Cerberus was working on than her. It was also nice just to be able to sit back and let someone else do the heavy lifting. It had been a long time since anyone had done that for her.

Coltraine had been right when he accused her of not believing in happy endings. She'd stopped believing when her father had died and left her with her wicked stepmother, who'd shipped her off to boarding school before her father's corpse had a chance to grow cold. By the time she came of age to access her inheritance, most of it had been embezzled by her father's solicitor, who was now married to her stepmother.

The inheritance hadn't been a lot, Samantha had used it to purchase her small cottage outside of London and then had found work as a bartender. The money hadn't been bad, especially with the tips and private gigs she'd been able to land. She'd begun writing on the side, hoping to be able to provide a few better-quality necessities. Saving for everything had made her frugal and she'd opted to become an online gamer for recreation.

Once she and her friends won the prize for the Castle Reign real-life game, she'd left bartending behind and become a full-time writer. Being able to devote herself to writing and honing her craft had enabled her to steadily advance her career to the point she no longer needed a day job.

Someone had told her that writing erotic romance had a stigma attached to it, and she knew several authors who'd been let go from their day jobs when their employers found out. So, when she started, she'd used a pen name. Once she didn't have to worry about an employer, she'd gone to using her real name as there was a certain thrill that came from seeing her own name on paperbacks or on e-versions of her books.

She'd fallen in love with the genre and been excited as her books had climbed up the various best seller lists and begun to really pay off. It hadn't always been easy; in fact, it had been difficult and often isolating, but she'd begun to earn more money than she had ever imagined possible.

"So, Ms. Butler, most respected authors write under a pen name. What made you decide to use your real one?"

"You don't have to answer that, Samantha. It's not germane to the case and isn't any of Detective Moore's business."

"It's okay, King," she said quietly, placing her hand on Coltraine's arm.

The testosterone in the room had been at lethal levels a couple of times, and if answering Moore's snide question would help lessen the tension, she had no objection.

"When I started, I did start with a pen name, but once I could write full time, I switched to my real name. I had no idea that people would look down on what I wrote or that a lot of authors use pen names for safety. It never occurred to me that some whack job would come after me."

"What makes you think he's a whack job?" Moore asked belligerently.

Coltraine placed his hand on hers. "Because he's stalking our client and killed one of our employees. Royce? Get this asshole out of here."

"You can't throw me out," snarled Moore.

"I wouldn't make a bet on that if I were you," said Royce, pulling the detective's chair back. "You were allowed in as a courtesy. The way you've treated our client, who has done nothing wrong, is deplorable. Dillon, you're welcome to stay and ask questions but be advised you're skating on thin ice."

Royce hustled Moore down the stairs and then stood in front of them, preventing the detective from using them.

"Care to share anything about Jen's death that your partner seemed to want to withhold?" asked Coltraine.

"The department's official line is that we can't comment on ongoing investigations, but…" he said, holding up his hand, "I know she was one of your employees and most likely was doing something for your client."

Coltraine nodded. "There was no reason to think she would be in any danger. She's been training with us since we established the office here and before that had trained to be a volunteer deputy in her hometown. Samantha left a bag with her clothing in the locker, and Jen was dispatched to pick it up."

"That's all we found… toiletry items, as well as clothing. No evidence of a laptop, cell, or other electronic devices."

"I kept them with me. My laptop is my life. It never leaves my side."

Coltraine chuckled. "I can attest to that."

"The department would like to take a look at it, if possible," said Dillon.

"I'm afraid that won't be doable. If your people

will let us know what you're looking for, we will consider sending you copies. We will also forward you any further emails or messages. I believe you already have what we have."

"Is there any chance I can get my things back?" she asked.

"I'm afraid to say probably not. Moore is the senior detective on the case and given you won't give us your laptop and you tossed him out of this meeting, he'll probably hang onto them just for spite."

"Oh goody, corsets and thongs, it is," quipped Coltraine.

"Seth, if I make you a list…"

"I'll be happy to pick up whatever you need, although I'm not sure why. I think corsets and thongs are an excellent idea."

Samantha rolled her eyes. "Not at all practical. Do you know how hard it is to breathe in one of those things?"

Dillon smiled. "You know you can place yourself in police protective custody, but I doubt the accommodations will be anywhere near this nice."

"No, thank you. Cavemen for company notwithstanding, I prefer to trust my safety to Cerberus."

"Understood."

"When can we expect a copy of the full medical examiner and police reports?" asked Coltraine.

"Again, your non-cooperative manner has been duly noted. You're not making any friends at HQ."

"I think you'd be surprised the number of 'friends' Club Southside and Cerberus have within your department. As for our cooperation, we supplied you with a positive ID for Jen and took care of notification to the family. We've given you copies of all the messages and emails sent to our client and even the results of where we traced them back to. We allowed you access to our client. Let me remind you, Detective Dillon, none of those were things we had to do. We did it to be cooperative. You don't want to share? Fine, we'll start looking for Jen's killer ourselves. We'll try not to step on your toes while we're doing it."

"It's okay, King," she said quietly to him.

"It's not okay, Samantha. You were right not to go to them. They would have been less helpful and probably far less polite than the cops in England. Royce talked to some of our friends at HQ. Moore has been written up for shoddy police work more than once. And Dillon here just got promoted from patrol to detective. This is his first case."

"Then why did Moore let Dillon take the lead in questioning?" asked Samantha.

"Because Moore is just putting in his time. He doesn't give a shit," said King.

"In other words," added Seth, "they assigned you the bottom of the barrel."

Dillon at least had the grace to look shamefaced. "I'll see if I can't do something about your things."

"This is how green he is. He can't. They were part of a murder scene and will be needed for evidence. At the very least, they're going to need to be processed. Seth, show Detective Dillon to the door. If you have further questions, you can submit them to Cerberus."

"You can't keep your client from us if we want to talk to her."

"Sure, we can. We can either get any warrant you obtain quashed, or we can simply leave the country."

Detective Dillon sputtered as Seth steered him out the door and down the stairs. There seemed to be a bit of a scuffle as the two detectives puffed themselves up to argue with Seth and Royce.

Coltraine pulled his cell out of his pocket, pointing to the screen, "That's not going to get them anywhere. Coltraine," he answered the cell. "Yeah, Harvey, what can I do for you?"

[Indistinct talking]

"I understand that. But your department assigned a guy who's just doing time until he's pensioned off and a rookie who's so green it hurts. They wanted to play whose dick is bigger. They lost."

[Indistinct talking]

Coltraine laughed. "A personal favor, huh? That could come in useful. We'll let them back up, but you tell them to play nice or next time we'll kick their asses down the stairs, not escort them in a professional manner."

[Indistinct talking]

"Hockey tickets? Nah, I'm going to want so much more for giving your detectives a second chance."

Coltraine ended the call and hit a button on the console. "Seth? Royce? As a favor to Chicago PD because they asked so nice, we're going to give Tweedle Dumb and Tweedle Dumber a second chance."

"You're enjoying this," Samantha accused.

"Yes, but I'm also setting the parameters of how Chicago PD is going to interact with Cerberus. We can be of great help to them. There are things we can do and information we can get that they can't. But we aren't going to take their shit."

The two detectives marched back in with Seth and Royce behind them.

"I saw Detective Moore take a call—by the way, had we wanted to, we could have jammed it. I take it you've been instructed as to how to conduct yourselves?"

"Yeah, but just because you have some of the brass in your pocket doesn't mean you'll always get your way," grumbled Moore.

"I don't know what your problem is Moore, but if you fuck this up or treat our client with anything other than the utmost courtesy, I'm going to make it one of my personal goals in life to make the time you have left to retirement as unpleasant as I possibly can."

"You can't just demand things from us and not give anything in return," said Dillon.

"That's not what we did… at least not at first. It's become obvious to my team that you aren't inclined to treat the threat to Samantha seriously."

"Maybe not," said Dillon, grudgingly. "But I can assure you we take the murder of Jennifer Kelly very seriously. You seem convinced that her murder is tied to the problems Ms. Butler is having."

"I don't have 'problems' Detective; I'm being stalked," she said, frustrated.

"Take it easy, baby. They don't get it, and they don't have to. It'll keep us from having to trip over them."

"If you interfere in our investigation…" started the ever-belligerent Moore.

"Just what is it you think you'll do?" asked Coltraine in a deceptively calm voice. "Because I can tell you what we'll do. We'll solve both cases and make your department look incompetent. The press will have a field day. Trust me, when we're through, Samantha will be the poor, mistreated victim, which she is, and your department will throw you two under the bus."

"Can we just take a step back?" said Dillon. "We really didn't even know about the stalking complaints, as she never came to us. And I don't blame her. It sounds like you got the bum's rush in England. Our laws here in the States aren't very effective until the unsub actually does something physical and by then it's often too late. At least we have a copy of the threats, and any additional information you can give us would be appreciated."

"What should be clear is this psycho is escalating. I realize you don't necessarily believe that, but we do. We will keep Samantha safe."

"Have you thought about just kind of going underground for a while, Ms. Butler. Maybe let Chicago PD and Cerberus do their jobs while you play it safe?"

"What the hell do you think I should do? I'm confined to a safe house in a foreign country guarded by some of the best people in the security business. Exactly where is it you think I'd be safer?" snarled Samantha.

"There's no need to bite his head off, baby," said Coltraine before turning on Dillon. "You may not believe you could keep her safe, which I would tend to agree with, but Cerberus can and will. No lunatic killer is going to make Samantha run and hide from him. If he wants her, he'll go through us. In case you missed it, detectives, our client is also a victim. She has done nothing wrong."

"Well, her books aren't exactly great literature," grumped Moore.

"Maybe not, but only time will tell that complete tale," said Samantha. "All I know is I get letters, emails, and messages every day from women telling me my book changed their lives for the better. I didn't start out thinking they were anything more than salacious entertainment, but I've come to understand they mean so much more than that to so many of my readers. You don't like them? Fine. Nobody's putting a gun to your head to read them. But I'll be damned if you or anyone else is going to tell me I can't write them."

"You tell 'em, baby," Coltraine said with pride in his voice.

"But until we can prove that your client is actually a victim of a stalker and that the two cases are related, we will focus our investigation on the murder," said Moore.

"Get out," Coltraine said in a tone that brooked no defiance. "As I said, if you want to talk to our client, you will go through us. If you don't like that, tough shit." He stood up, towering over the two detectives. "Come on, baby. You and I will go upstairs while Royce and Seth make sure these two stooges leave our building."

He offered her his hand and she took it, liking the way it felt to have him wrap his arm around her and escort her to the vintage elevator. Samantha had never had anyone stick up for her... ever. Even her father had made excuses for her stepmother and from the day he'd died, Samantha had felt as if she were on her own.

All of the tension fell away as she realized that was no longer true. She had her very own hero and if she wanted a happily ever after, it was hers for the taking.

CHAPTER 15

SAMANTHA

The next few days fell into a lovely kind of routine. She spent her nights reveling in Coltraine's arms and her days continuing her everyday existence as a romance writer. Only now, she was not alone; she was taken care of and stretch breaks were often really sex breaks. It was the most marvelous way to spend her time. Interestingly enough, even though she took more breaks than ever before, she actually got more done. She supposed it was because sex actually seemed to revive her entire being.

Samantha had made a list of items she would need, and Seth had been dispatched to procure them. He had a well-developed sense of fashion and for the most part, she'd been pleased with the purchases. The exception was in undergarments. He had refused to buy her panties, which Coltraine had openly encouraged, and her request for 'suitable, serviceable' bras had been ignored. Oh, they were supportive enough and in fact were comfortable, but short of her club wear, she'd never owned such sexy bras in her whole life.

Seth and Royce seemed to welcome her into the fold and acted as if she and Coltraine had been together forever. It often felt like that to Samantha as well, but she reminded herself it hadn't been any time at all and they were in a kind of pressure cooker situation. For the most part, Seth and Royce stayed down on the second floor after she and Coltraine locked themselves away on the third floor and they'd swept the building. During the day, Coltraine set her up in his office and worked either in there with her or in the war room.

In London, Sully and Nina continued to coordinate with Seth to see if they could run down her assailant's identity. The Chicago PD kept them apprised of their progress in finding Jen's killer, but seemed to be getting nowhere. Part of the problem was that they didn't seem to be interested in linking the two cases together. Like the team at Cerberus, Samantha was convinced that was a mistake.

The nights were like the very best parts of her steamy novels. Kingston Coltraine could take her places she'd never even dreamed of going. From the moment she had allowed herself to believe that there could be a happily ever after with Coltraine, her happiness had seemed to expand exponentially. With him she felt confident, sexy, and optimistic. The dark cloud, that had often seemed to hang over her head, disappeared.

More than once, Coltraine's hand had caressed her backside. She had to admit, she liked it. She often ate her meals sitting in his lap with him feeding her. She liked it when he fed her and even though he was a solid slab of muscle, she found him easy to cuddle up with—in bed or out. When they fucked, there was plenty of pleasure, but he'd taught her that she liked more than a little bite of pain alongside it. As for male sexual dominance? She was a big fan.

While inside the bedroom he was all about control and domination, outside of it he was caring and seemed to genuinely enjoy doing things for her. For herself, she began to enjoy taking care of him, doing things that made his life a little easier and oh, how she loved being submissive to him in matters of sex.

Coltraine had been loath to leave her but had wanted to follow up on something personally. Royce was out running down a lead, which left Samantha alone with Seth. Seth Newcomb was an interesting fellow. Of the three, he was probably the most classically handsome and had a little boy smile that could light up a room. He was funny and playful, but she sensed there was a darkness and strength that lurked within the sunny façade.

Having just finished a chapter, Samantha pushed

back from the desk and stretched her arms overhead. She heard Seth moving around and made him a cup of coffee. With two steaming mugs, she joined him at his desk in the bullpen.

"Thank you," he said. "You're so quiet and easy to be around, I sometimes forget you're even here. When I do remember it, I have to remind myself that it hasn't been for that long."

Samantha nodded. "I completely understand. I feel the same way, which is weird because I have spent most of my adult life either alone or online. Before all this started, there were weeks that I wouldn't even leave my cottage."

"Cottage? Such a quintessentially English term. I picture this quaint little home with a short stone wall, a lovely garden, and thatch roof."

"You're not far off, but before you get visions of my green thumb, I feel compelled to tell you that I have a gardener, and a housecleaner who comes in twice a month."

Seth grinned. "I hate to break it to you, but King's home is an enormous, industrial loft with a killer view of the lake on one side and the city's skyline on the other." He paused as if he was considering his next words, carefully. "I had my doubts about keeping you here and about you and King in general, but I was wrong. I never should have doubted King's instincts and now I wonder why anyone who got to know you would doubt your veracity about the unsub. I can't believe the cops in England, and here for that matter, blew you off."

"They think it's a publicity stunt."

"It isn't. And even if they could convince themselves you'd written the messages, why wouldn't you have made the public aware? I mean, if it was for the publicity, you'd need to be milking it in the press and in social media. No. They're just lazy dumb shits. Sometimes I watch you and King, and it feels like you two have been together forever. Almost as if you were inevitable."

Feeling a little cornered, Samantha said, "We're not that serious. Just something to while away the time."

The look Seth shot her said he didn't buy her line of bullshit. Even though she wanted to believe more than she'd ever wanted anything, her past experience just kept coming up to plague her, filling her head with moments of doubt.

"I don't believe that's true for you," he said regarding her over the rim of his mug. "And I've known King long enough to know that it isn't at all true for him."

"I'm convenient."

Seth shook his head, chuckling. "I call dibs on being there when you tell *him* that and he paints your ass all kinds of red."

"You're a Dom…"

"You just now figuring that out?" he laughed.

"Guess I'm going to have to boost my testosterone or make my leathers fit tighter."

Of the three, he was by far the easiest-going. It was easy to accept him at face value—pretty face, great body, well-dressed and with an amiable nature. But Samantha was learning there was more than one way to be a dominant alpha male.

"I hate to sound like I'm in high school, but do you really think he likes me?" she asked quietly.

The second the words were out, she wished she could call them back, or better yet, have never said them at all. She felt silly for having said them but couldn't help but hold her breath as she waited for Seth to answer. After all, he'd known Coltraine far longer than she had.

"Let me put it this way," Seth said with a grin. "I think it's better that you asked me that question instead of him. Kingston Coltraine never loses control… I mean ever. He's happy to top a sub who wants a session, but he doesn't engage with them on an emotional level. He can sit next to what other people say is the hottest, sexiest woman who ever lived and not have it affect him. By the way—that's you, as far as he's concerned. If he isn't physically touching you, he's following you with his eyes—not in a creepy, stalker way. And he sure as hell doesn't haul other women into his lap so he can feed them."

Samantha couldn't quite contain the smile she could feel lifting the corners of her mouth. "I do like that. I never thought I would. I used to watch Fitz haul JJ into his lap and feed her or have her sit between his legs so he could stroke her hair. I always wondered what either of them got out of that. JJ is the strongest woman I know, and yet she practically purrs at Fitz when he touches her, and not in an icky kind of way. I never understood it until I met King."

"Fitz is a good man; so is King. There are few better. I'm not saying he won't fuck up because he will, and if I know King it will be spectacular. But my advice is to stay the course with him, and he'll put things right. He meant what he said, Samantha. He'll keep you safe. Not because you're our client and that's his job. Not because you're some damsel in distress being stalked by an asshole and that calls to his knight in shining armor. No. King will keep you safe because you're his woman and he couldn't do anything else. Don't get used to that little training collar he put around your neck the other day."

She reached up to touch the braided silver collar. Tears had threatened to fall when Coltraine had placed it around her neck. He assured her it was temporary and just for show.

Samantha shook her head. "I know it's just one that the club plans to use and doesn't mean anything. It'll just make it easier for people to accept me as part of his life for now."

Seth laughed again. "You are in for such a spanking if he ever learns of this conversation. I'm going to be able to blackmail you for years with this shit. That simple plain collar is temporary. He wants it there to remind not only you, but Royce and me and anyone else who ventures in here, that you are unavailable. I have a sneaky suspicion he has something far more luxurious and far more permanent in mind, with a ring to match. You do know at Cerberus in London that all of the guys try to outdo the collar and ring Fitz gave JJ? Most of them don't have the money it takes to do that. Well, all except Nigel, and I do think he managed to pull it off."

Samantha was stunned and stuck between wanting to believe Seth and wanting to keep her heart safe. But why would Seth lie? She wanted to keep some small part of her being that hadn't already committed itself to Coltraine separate, so that if it all fell apart, she'd at least have something left of herself. She tried to think what body part that might be. The tip of her nose? No, he kissed that far too often. Her ear lobe? No, he liked to nip that when he nuzzled her neck. Well, that left her neck out, too. Her pussy, clit, nipples, labia, and ass had all given over that first night. The problem was, he'd turned her entire body into his personal playground, and she reveled in his attention. She'd never felt sexier, nor had she ever written such steamy, explicit prose.

"You aren't just saying that so I'll be a good little client sub, are you?"

"You'll be a 'good little client sub' because not

being one will get you into all kinds of trouble with your Dom. But for the record, no. I'm telling you because I like you. I never thought a woman would come along who could destroy King, but you could. If you're playing him, and I don't think you are…"

"But Royce does." It wasn't a question, and she really didn't say it with any rancor. It just was the way things were. Royce was unfailingly polite, but there was something she couldn't quite put her finger on.

"Royce doesn't count," Seth said dismissively. "Look, not to be telling tales, but Royce got badly hurt emotionally a couple of years ago. He doesn't trust anybody… most of all himself. He might trust us to have his back and haul his ass out of hell, but there's a piece of Royce that died and I'm not sure he'll ever get it back. But as I said, just take care of King. He has been through hell and crawled his way back into the light."

"The scars…"

Seth nodded. "Yeah. My two best friends are covered in them. One has scars all over his body from where some bastards tortured him. The other has scars on the inside that he inflicted himself."

"What about you?" she said with a tilt of her chin.

"Me? I'm fucking perfect."

She leaned over and kissed the top of his head. "Yes, you are. Unfortunately for you, I think I'm falling in love with this other brutally handsome, uber-dominant alpha male."

"Just like the kind you write about in your books."

"How would you know?" she teased.

"Are you kidding? The women at Baker Street love your and Sage's books. I understand there's a whole library of them and some others in the submissives' lounge. Apparently, JJ likes them because neither of you write wimpy girls who need someone else to save them. I figured reading them would give me the inside scoop as to what they were looking for."

Samantha laughed. "The problem with your theory is what a woman wants in her book boyfriend often has little to do with what she wants in her real life one. The first book I ever wrote, I submitted to a niche publisher. He told me it was a good book, but I needed to change the heroine to a nineteen-year-old virgin. I told him it had been a long time since I'd been nineteen and even longer since I'd been a virgin."

"Did you change it?"

"I had it edited, commissioned a cover for it, and published it myself."

Seth cocked his head to one side. "If he ever really fucks up, forget what I said. Leave his sorry ass and come to me."

He stood up and before she knew what he was about, he pulled her into his arms and brushed his lips over hers. Her body registered a man who knew how to kiss, but her heart and soul rejected him. Seth was gorgeous and sexy, but he wasn't Coltraine. Had

Coltraine ruined her for anyone else? If Seth was right, did it even matter, as she would need no one else?

Seth's kiss didn't have Coltraine's fire or passion; it was almost clinical, as if he were trying to discern what Coltraine saw in her that had caused, according to Seth, such a radical change in the man. It might be a kind of unemotional experimentation for Seth, but for Samantha, it was just all kinds of wrong.

She bit Seth's lip at the same time she stomped on his instep. She would have done more, but the moment she let go of his lip with her teeth, he was jerked away and Coltraine's fist landed in his face. Samantha was prepared for him to be angry and to accuse her of something.

"You're an asshole, Newcomb," he growled menacingly before turning to her and touching her cheek reverently. "Are you all right, baby?"

CHAPTER 16

KING

Waking up next to Samantha, drawing her underneath him and making love to her first thing in the morning was the best. Better than all the other sex, even better than coffee, and for King that was saying something. He wasn't overly fond of waking without her right beside him, but hearing the shower running only made him want to get up and join her in there. Come to think of it, shower sex outranked coffee as well. In fact, sex with Samantha outweighed pretty much everything.

Even the actual sleep he got with Samantha was better. Many nights since he'd been renditioned, true, deep sleep had been elusive, but with Samantha, he made love to her and then curled around her and found the kind of peaceful sleep men like him only dreamed about.

He swung his legs over the bed when his cell

vibrated. He looked down. Dillon. What did that asshole want? King had never been a big fan of the Chicago PD or cops in general, but Dillon and his less-than-useless partner, Moore, were becoming a thorn in his side. Cerberus had begun their own investigation into Jen's death as they no longer believed Dillon and Moore were up to the job.

"What?" King answered the phone without any preliminaries.

"I know you're pissed, and I don't blame you…" Dillon started.

"Good. Then you'll understand why I'm ending this call."

"Coltraine. King. Please, don't. Can you meet me for breakfast at Elmo's Diner?"

"How the hell does a fresh-face rookie know about Elmo's?"

Elmo's was an old-fashioned diner in one of the rougher neighborhoods in Chicago. Sex workers, pimps, drug dealers, and the like ate there. The one rule was the diner and its surrounding area was neutral territory for anyone eating there. King wasn't convinced that the United Nations wouldn't be better off disbanding and letting Elmo run the peacekeeping efforts of the world. Nobody broke Elmo's rule. Anybody who did never had the chance to do it again. But the food was great.

"That used to be my patrol beat. It's where I overheard information that allowed me to make a big bust on the other side of town and make detective. I know you guys aren't pleased with us and think we're stonewalling."

"Aren't you?"

"They are. I'm not. As you pointed out, Ms. Kelly deserves justice and if you believe her death is linked to Ms. Butler, I'm willing to go along."

"The Blue Shield isn't going to like you talking to me. You could find yourself without a partner or back-up."

"I'm willing to risk that. I didn't become a cop to solve easy cases and wait for retirement."

"Then why did you?"

"Corny as it sounds, to serve and protect."

King chuckled. "Dudley Do-Right."

He was surprised to hear an echoing and self-deprecating laugh from the other end of the line. "I've been accused of worse. But it's true. I got into law enforcement because I thought I could make a difference. This case is being back-burnered and not just by Moore. The pressure is coming from up top. I want to know who and why and find Ms. Kelly's killer."

Making his mind up that perhaps the kid was worth knowing, King said, "What time?"

"Will nine work for you?"

"I can make it work. I have a couple of other things I need to do today. I'll see you then."

Not only could he smell Samantha when she walked out of the bath, he could feel her. He looked up and smiled. "New rule: don't leave our bed without telling me. I don't like waking up without you."

"You're a controlling sonofabitch," she said, smiling.

"Not true. My mother is a lovely person. I, however, take after my father who can be a real bastard."

She shook her head, laughing. As he stood and crossed to her, she opened up the towel she'd had wrapped around her and welcomed him into her space. He couldn't bring himself to say the three little words he wanted to. Not because he was afraid to say them, but because he feared she was. Samantha wrote about romance and happy endings, but she was afraid to believe in them.

He wrapped his arms around her, letting his morning wood throb between them. "See? If you'd woken me up, you could have taken care of this thing. Now, I have to shove it into a pair of jeans before I head out onto the mean streets of Chicago."

"Oh? Where are we going?"

"I am going to go run a few errands and follow up on a lead. You are going to go work on finishing your novel so that it gets to your poor editor on time."

"She doesn't mind."

"She does, but doesn't want to hurt your feelings or offend her best client. And honestly, I am not as concerned with her as I am with how stressed you get."

"I'm not stressed."

"Yes, you are. You're writing dialog in your sleep."

"I am not."

He laughed. "You do, but it's kind of cute. Once I realized you weren't talking to some ex-lover I was fine with it."

She arched her eyebrow at him. "I don't believe you're jealous. You are far too full of yourself to be insecure."

"Maybe, but you're right. I'm not jealous. That would imply I don't trust you, which couldn't be further from the truth. The fact is, I'm territorial as all get out, so be prepared when we're down in the club. I might want you on display and other guys can look, but I'll deck any man who tries to touch what's mine."

He kissed her lightly and turned away before he decided that Detective Dillon could keep his information to himself, and he'd fuck Samantha instead. His dick agreed that was a much better plan.

"And am I?" she asked with almost heartbreaking sincerity. "Yours, I mean."

"How about we talk that through tonight with you draped over my lap getting your ass paddled for even thinking about doubting it."

That seemed to help settle something in her. Every time he thought that she had begun to believe absolutely, doubt began to creep in. If he ever found the guy or guys who had made her gun shy, King intended to rearrange their faces.

"How about if I take your word for it?"

"How about if I spank you anyway because you get so wet when I do?"

"That isn't true…"

"Isn't it?" he asked. "My guess is your pussy is already softening and getting primed for me even knowing it'll be a while."

King came back to her, dropping to his knees and nuzzling her sex, before letting his tongue dart out to flick her clit and take a swipe through her labia. He looked up to see her nipples were beading, and not from the cold. "That ought to help that sex scene you were having trouble with last night."

Samantha laughed. "You're terrible. I don't know why…"

"Why what, Samantha?"

He watched as a myriad of emotions swirled in her eyes. King was afraid she was going to take another step back.

"Why I seem to find myself falling for you," she said with an inhaled breath.

He stood and wrapped his arms around her. "That's all right, baby. It's okay to fall; I'll catch you when you do." He hugged her tight and then let go, turning her around and giving her luscious backside a swat. "Go get dressed; go to work; and behave yourself. I'll stop somewhere special and bring you back something for lunch."

"That sounds good. Any chance we can eat in our room?"

"Only if you sit in my lap naked and let me feed you," he said with a deliberate leer.

"That's what I had in mind," she said coquettishly.

His dick thumped hard against the closed fly of his jeans.

Oh, I am so fucking her when I get back. Dillon better have something worthwhile.

King headed out of the building, deliberately turning away from the direction he meant to go. The hairs on the back of his neck stood up and he felt as though someone had eyes on him. Both Royce and Seth had reported they felt they were being watched but had nothing substantial to base it on. He set a good pace but ensured that it didn't look like he was rushing to get anywhere. He hopped a bus and got off three stops later, lingering as he peered in the store windows, hoping to catch a glimpse of who might be following him.

It might be related to Samantha; it might not, but King wasn't taking any chances.

He slowed imperceptibly when he caught a glimpse of a reflection in the window—not there long enough for him to be able to identify the person, but enough of an impression to make him leave his other errands for another time. He would lead whoever it was on a merry goose chase and then leave them hanging when they least expected it, doubling back to make his appointment with Dillon.

As he walked, King continued to try and spot his tail. Maybe he was just being paranoid. Maybe he was on edge because he'd left Samantha in Seth's care. He knew she was safe; knew Seth would die for her; but then, Jen had died, and it hadn't stopped whoever it was from coming after her. He tried to tell himself he was just being paranoid, but where Samantha's safety was concerned, nothing seemed too cautious.

Samantha wasn't aware that she had not seen all of the emails that had been sent, as Sully and Nina had installed a filter on her server that routed everything to them first. King had made the decision to not tell her. He sure as hell hadn't asked her permission, but he'd also made it clear that Nina and Sully were only to intercept any emails that might be threatening or give them a clue to the unsub's identity.

Sully had reported the stalker's emails were ramping up. At first, he'd been angry and frustrated that it had been Jen he killed. Then he had escalated and told her that he knew she was in the Southside, and he would be coming for her, regardless of the number of bodyguards she hired. Sully's analysis was that the unsub thought the cops had her stashed away, but the concern was the threats were becoming more violent and vivid.

He forced himself to remain calm as he continued walking towards a destination only he knew. Even though his appearance might seem cool and collected, King's adrenaline began to pump, not in fear, but in anticipation. At last, it felt as though the game was really on. He ran up the stairs to the L train as it pulled into the station. He walked the length of the platform, surreptitiously watching it to see if anyone looked out of place or familiar. He waited until the last moment before barely making it onto the train as the doors closed.

That should do it. If his instincts had been correct, he should have evaded whoever was following him if there had been anyone at all. But King felt sure he was right. If it was the stalker, then he knew where Samantha was. They would need to bring in more people to ensure they were secure. But King's instincts told him that it wasn't the unsub. If Dillon was right, somewhere in the city, someone, for reasons unknown, was applying pressure and wanted to know what Cerberus knew. He or she might be able to keep tabs on what was happening with the police department, but they had no way of knowing what Cerberus knew, suspected, or what they were doing.

Had the stalker done this before? If so, had he targeted steamy romance writers alone, or had others offended his sense of morality? If Samantha was his first target, what had set him off and what had made him read her books in the first place? King regretted having allowed Samantha to know as much about the investigation as she did, but it was her safety at stake, and it was necessary to keep her safe. If she didn't follow the rules, he had a D/s contract that spelled out she had agreed to accept his authority and discipline.

He shook his head as he exited the train a few stops down and stopped, waiting for the platform to clear before going to the opposite end to head down the stairs. He didn't have any real interest in spanking Samantha for discipline. Oh, he wanted to spank her, but only in a way that lit her up and set her motor running.

So far, so good. The feeling of being watched had left him, but he made a circuitous route to Elmo's anyway. So far, he, Seth, and Royce had been able to handle everything; it might be time to officially open Cerberus and the club for business. They couldn't put it off indefinitely, and he would ensure nothing happened to Samantha.

The sonofabitch had managed to slip away. The city's cameras would pick him up again. If nothing else, Samantha Butler's location had been ascertained. Detective Dillon had been careful not to mention where Cerberus had Butler stashed, but Moore hadn't been nearly as careful.

If the detectives got in the way, Dillon would have to be dealt with. Moore would just happily fade into retirement and the bottle. Dillon was one of those do-gooder cops. If Samantha Butler was killed on his watch, the dumb rookie would stop at nothing to track down the killer. That could not be allowed to happen. He would keep on as he always had, but Samantha Butler must die.

CHAPTER 17

KING

King was impressed. As he entered the diner, Detective Dillon was waiting for him in the back, away from a window. It wasn't easy to score one of the back tables. Maybe the kid was smarter or better trained than he'd first believed. He seemed a bit nervous, but then their last verbal exchange hadn't been exactly friendly.

"I didn't know whether to order or not. I wasn't sure if we were actually having breakfast…"

"The first thing you're going to do is change seats with me. I never sit with my back to the room. And I don't know or care about you, but I'm having breakfast. I didn't have time to eat any food before I left Samantha naked in our room…"

The detective blushed, which was oddly amusing in a grown ass man, but obligingly moved, and King sank down into the comfy booth, leaving the detective to sit in the chairs with his back to the room.

"You can't sleep with a client."

"No, kid. You can't sleep with someone you're protecting. I'm sure there are all kinds of rules prohibiting that, but in my case, I'm black ops security personnel, and when my client is the sexiest thing on two legs, I can do whatever I like."

King sat back, laying his arm along the back of the booth.

"Ms. Butler seems like a lovely person…"

"Is that why you let your partner treat her like shit? Because in case you missed it, I care deeply about our client on a personal level. I will do whatever it takes to keep her safe regardless of what you, your partner, or the Chicago PD think about it."

Interesting.

When the Chicago PD was mentioned, the kid had gone a little pale.

"Why don't you tell me why you called me down here? I'm fairly sure meeting with me this morning is against regulations and yet you felt compelled to do it. That tells me your partner may be a douchebag, but there's hope for you."

"Thanks, I think," said Dillon nervously. "Cards on the table?"

"Either yours are, or I'm headed back to Cerberus. I very much doubt mine will be except in the most vague of terms."

"God, you're a real hard ass, aren't you?"

"When the guys who are supposed to be on your side rendition you to someplace where they like to stick hot pokers in you, you tend to lose your faith in those guys. These days I trust my team and Samantha. That's it."

Dillon sat back. "You really care about her."

"Not that it's any of your fucking business, but I love her. Jesus, I can't believe I just told you that. Do me a favor and don't ever mention that to Samantha. I think she'd probably prefer it if I told her first."

"Probably, and my lips are sealed. I'm just glad to hear you think I may be in the position of telling her someday."

"So much for my oversharing. Why did you bring me down here?"

"You're right. The investigation has stalled out—not because I'm not trying to follow up. Even Moore was trying in the beginning, but you're right—he doesn't want to rock the boat this close to retirement."

"What about you?"

"I'm a long way from retirement. Requests for basic assistance like forensics were either outright denied or moved to very low on the totem pole. And with the amount of crime that happens in this city, low priority means no priority and it just gets shuffled away."

Interesting. Maybe the kid could be useful.

King sat forward and then back as the waitress came to take their order.

"Hey, King," she said with a smile. "I hear the club is getting ready to have an exclusive, invitation only event. Any chance you need a server for the night?"

King nodded. "I think that can be arranged. You looking to become a member?"

The young waitress blushed. "I don't know that I could afford it or even if I'm really interested, but I read a lot of books about clubs and if nothing else, I'd like to see it. Everyone's talking about it. I hope you've got good security."

"The best, and Club Southside will be like Elmo's—neutral territory. But yeah, leave me your number and I'll see what I can do."

"I'd be happy to give you my number whether you can get me in or not."

King shook his head. "Turn your charms on the detective…"

"Shit, don't tell them who I am."

Both King and the waitress laughed. "Kid, before you had a seat, they knew who you were. But Elmo's is safe. No one violates its neutrality."

King turned back to the waitress. "As for why you should bat those big, beautiful eyes at Dillon here, it would be because I have a set of big blue ones waiting for me."

"Damn," she said. "Are you telling me Kingston

Coltraine is off the market?"

"Yes, and happily so."

"Well, that's disappointing. I was told you were a whip master, with the ones with all the string thingies on the end."

King laughed. "That's called a flogger, and I am. Whether my beloved will be okay with me offering sessions to needy subs that don't include aftercare of any kind remains to be seen, but I'm not the only one who's good with a whip or flogger. I tell you what. Why don't you find appropriate fet wear for the club and I'll put your name on the guest list."

"Could you? That'd be awfully nice."

"Consider it done."

"So, what would you gents like," she asked.

"I'll have a Denver omelet with hashbrowns and white toast," said Dillon.

"God, could you get any more cliché? I'll take Joe's Special with extra parmesan and an English muffin, lots of butter."

"Done and done. Should I bring a carafe of coffee or just fill your mugs?"

The waitress was a pretty little thing. She seemed to have a submissive streak. She might be a great addition to the club. Finding good submissives was key to having a great club and finding them was more difficult than some might think. But then, finding a good Dom could be just as difficult.

"French press for me," said King, looking across to

Dillon, "unless you like that weak stuff they serve everyone else."

"I'm good with the French press and cancel my order. I'll have what he's having."

King chuckled; Detective Dillon might turn into a first-rate contact at the police department.

"So, it's not that you're stonewalling us; you're being stonewalled by somebody in your department. Interesting. Can you tell where the pressure's coming from?"

"High up, as in higher up than just our precinct. There was a time Moore was a good cop, but now he just goes along with things. He was actually doing decent work and then just backed off. When I asked why, he told me to mind my own business and let it go into the unsolved homicides. They'll note it as random violence and that'll be the end of it."

"That doesn't sound like the worst advice," said King.

"Are you kidding? It's terrible advice. Jennifer Kelly wasn't even in her thirties. She had a whole life to live, and somebody snuffed it out. Whether or not it's connected to your client is irrelevant. Moore and I also took some heat about Butler writing porn and were told that maybe she should just lie low and go back to England."

"Yeah, because their police treated her so much better. You really want to find Jen some justice, don't you, Do-Right?"

The way Dillon grinned; King knew it wasn't the first time someone had called him that.

"Yeah," he said, shaking his head. "I do, and if that means going off the books and doing it on my own time, I will."

"They'll fire you for that kind of shit."

"I don't much care. I want her folks to know her killer was caught and made to pay."

King nodded. "Okay, kid, I believe you. I'm going to tell you what we've learned and if this gets back to the wrong people, you will have burned your bridges with Cerberus forever."

"I know you have no reason to, but I swear you can trust me."

The waitress returned and placed their plates in front of them. The kid's eyes got a bit wider, but he didn't say anything.

"Don't worry, Dillon. It's eggs, ground beef, spinach, potatoes, onions, peppers, and parmesan. Looks kind of disgusting, but it's delicious. It's one of the ways people at Elmo's know you're in the know. It's not on the menu."

Dillon took a bite, hesitantly at first and then savoring it as the delicious taste spread in his mouth. "That is delicious. Remind me to let you order for me in the future."

"Then I hope you like your scotch neat, old, and expensive."

Dillon laughed. "I've never had anything harder than beer."

"Where you from, Do-Right?"

"Kansas—Dodge City to be exact."

King started to laugh. "I probably don't want to know this, but your first name wouldn't be Matt, would it?"

The detective looked chagrined. "I'm afraid so. The damn show went off the air before I was born."

"Yes, but it will live on in reruns and streaming forever. Just do yourself a favor and never date a girl called Kitty or get assigned to a partner named Festus."

"Duly noted."

"By the way, what I'm about to tell you is truly need to know, and I have determined Samantha doesn't need to know."

"Got it."

"Our IT people are located in the London office…"

"Atop another sex club, right?"

"Okay, here's the thing. Those of us in the lifestyle don't call them 'sex clubs,' although I admit there are some that operate that way. There's more involved with BDSM or D/s than just sex… so much more. But in answer to your question, yes. Cerberus has the top floor of the building that houses Baker Street in London. Baker Street and Cerberus proved to work well in the same building, so when JJ wanted to open a lifestyle club here in the States, Adam Wheldon agreed to run it for her if she agreed to put it in Chicago. Then Fitz announced we were opening another office here in Chicago. Anytime you're interested, I'll set you up with a guest pass."

"I can tell you the brass is none too pleased about it."

"Don't kid yourself. Some of the first people to apply are part of Chicago's elite. It's not for every-body, but don't knock it until you've at least learned more. In any event, I had our people install a filter on Samantha's email so that any kind of threat or nasty email goes to them instead of Samantha."

"She's your submissive, right? Doesn't she have to do whatever you tell her?"

King laughed. "Boy, have you got a lot to learn. In theory, she trusts me enough to make those decisions. In practice it gets a whole lot stickier and takes a bit of negotiation. They call it a power exchange. It's not one-sided… at least not in the relationships I want to mimic. And before you go off thinking submissives are weak? Some of the strongest people I know iden-tify as submissive."

"So have any more threats come through?"

"They have," said King, drawing out a stack of papers neatly folded in half. "And they aren't pretty. The unsub is now blaming Samantha, not only for whatever he thinks she did to him, but for forcing the sonofabitch to kill Jen. The last one is calling this bull-shit a crusade for morality and justice…"

"Delusions of grandeur."

King nodded. "Sully thinks, interestingly enough, that the emails are originating here in Chicago."

"Well, obviously he followed her…"

"No. Sully says they originated from here from the beginning. We're combing flight manifests." He held up his hand, "Don't go there. We're looking to see if we can spot someone making frequent trips. Right now, it's from when they started, but that's months and tens of thousands of people. But Sully is hoping they can narrow it down."

"So, it makes sense that we're getting pressure from above. Chicago is an 'old boys' network' kind of town. Someone is probably putting pressure on the mayor's or police commissioner's office."

"Or, it's someone in one of those offices."

The way Dillon sat back, King could see that possibility had never occurred to him.

"We don't know anything yet, but knowing you're getting pressure from above helps us start to narrow things down."

"I have to tell you, I'm feeling a whole lot better about all of this. I was really worried about Ms. Butler, but I don't think I need to concern myself with her safety."

"No, but although Elmo's is considered neutral, it

wouldn't be good for people seeing you coming and going from this block."

"I could come to Cerberus…"

"Not without a good reason."

"I could be applying for membership. I know you keep that strictly confidential, but don't the CCTV cameras pick up the comings and goings?"

King grinned. "Only after we've had a chance to scrub it so those coming in and out of the building can't be identified. But your idea for membership could work on a variety of levels. We're having an exclusive gala this Friday, with the grand opening to follow next week. If you're interested, email me and I'll send you an application and list of what you'll need."

"Should I get a new email address?"

"I wouldn't. You want this to look as normal as possible. I wouldn't use your police department email, but if you have a personal one that you normally use, go ahead and use that. That way everything looks like it's on the up and up."

"Should I tell people I'm joining?"

"I wouldn't. Most people don't want others knowing they're joining a sex club."

"You said it wasn't… oh, I get it—pull Dudley Do-Right's leg."

"You know kid, you're catching on. I'll pay the bill. No reason for anyone to see a charge from Elmo's on your credit card statement. You do know if this goes sideways, even if we catch the bad guy, this could hurt your career."

"I thought about that. What good is my career if it costs me what I believe in?"

"Well said, kid. Well said. See you Friday," said King.

He watched as Detective Dillon strode out the door, not seeming to have a care in the world, then touched the communication device in his ear. "Royce? You got him?"

"I'm on him, King."

There was trust and then there was trust. King's instincts said the detective could be trusted, but the last time he'd trusted an official ally, he had ended up being renditioned and tortured.

He wouldn't be making the same mistake again—particularly not with Samantha's life at stake.

CHAPTER 18

KING

King paid the bill, tipped the waitress heavily and headed back to Cerberus. He made his way back to the building, using a combination of buses and other ground transportation. He tried to avoid the subways when he could. There weren't many so it was usually easy to do. Too many years going down too many holes in the ground and having them blown up around him had made him wary.

When he was sure he was not being followed, he made his way to the first of two stops he wanted to make before returning. The first was to a custom corset shop on Chicago's famed Miracle Mile. It was the premier commercial area in the Windy City, maybe even the entire Midwest. It was a vibrant, bustling district containing upscale shops, restaurants, and hotels. Tucked into the back of one of the more luxe shops was a relatively unknown custom corsetiere known as Speak Easy. The shop was famous amongst those in the lifestyle with few shops that could compete—one in London and one in San Francisco among them.

King nodded to the clerk working the front end of the beautiful lingerie boutique and made his way into the corset shop.

"Mr. Coltraine, I have your items prepared."

"Thank you, Madame LaSalle. I knew I could count on you."

"She must be very special for you to surprise her with something this wonderful."

King knew that for Madame LaSalle, 'wonderful' translated to expensive. And it was, but as she held up the exquisite soft lavender leather corset with hand embroidered leaves and a matching thong, he couldn't bring himself to be sorry. Madame knew her colors. When King had sent her a picture of Samantha sleeping, she had suggested she had the perfect corset for her that could be cinched to fit her frame for the private gala event. King hoped that by the grand opening the following week, they would have dealt with the unsub, and he could have it personally fitted to her, as well as picking up several others.

Once he had that tucked into a discreet shopping bag, he headed a few doors down to one of the posh hotels and the exclusive jewelry store that resided within. Like with the Speak Easy, the store had a private room where certain clients could peruse some items not normally left in the cases for public consumption.

"Mr. Coltraine?" King nodded. "Right this way. I took the liberty of pulling a few pieces for you, but you, of course, are welcome to look at anything."

"I appreciate that," said King. "I'm in a bit of a hurry as I want to surprise Samantha, but I want it to be right."

"I believe you told me she isn't fond of yellow or warm golds, so I picked only those in white gold, platinum, and sterling silver."

King took the seat indicated and had to stop himself from gasping. With only a picture and a brief description of the woman for whom the items would be purchased, the man had done an outstanding job.

"I see you have excellent taste. I hate to warn you that this collar is perhaps the most expensive one we've ever been able to offer."

"I don't care. It's perfect for Samantha."

And it was— delicate strands of diamonds, seed pearls, and opals twisted together and around platinum beads to form a graceful rope. It was elegant, unique, and stunning… much like the woman herself.

"Any chance you have or can make an engagement ring for her and matching wedding bands? Mine needs to be channel set, as I work with my hands."

"We would be most happy to accommodate you. What do you want for the center stone?"

"Something rare and extraordinary."

"We have a white opal that would look stunning set in platinum and surrounded by diamonds running down the sides. I can have one of our artists send you some sketches, as well as pictures of the opals I suggest. It would be one of a kind."

"It sounds perfect. I'll take the collar with me and as soon as I see the sketches, I'll let you know on the ring."

"As you wish, sir."

Once he had the collar in a velvet pouch, he slipped it into his jeans pocket and headed out the door and back to Cerberus. Once there, he opened the front door with his key code. They had agreed after Jen was killed to lock down the building so only Royce, Seth, or King could admit someone inside. They were going to need to open up the building in the next day or so, though, as there were caterers and workers who needed to ready the club for both the exclusive gala as well as the grand opening. King knew Samantha was excited to attend, but he had yet to decide if she would be safe.

Just as he was calling for the elevator, his cell buzzed.

"Royce?"

"The kid is good," said Royce. "He made me about three blocks in. Once he doubled back on me, we took a walk through the park and talked. He showed me the copies of the emails you gave him.

This sucker is ramping up. Are you sure we want to have the gala event?"

"I think we have to. I just haven't decided if Samantha is coming or not. We can talk about it when you get back. I know Seth thinks we ought to make a big deal of it and even publicize that she will be there."

"I know you don't like it, but I think he's right," said Royce. "If we can secure her location, we might be able to draw the sonofabitch out, get him and put an end to this thing."

"I don't like the idea of offering Samantha up as bait. We already lost one woman; I'm not willing to lose another, but we can talk. I'll see you when you get back."

"I'll grab food for everybody."

"Sounds good." King ended the call.

King stepped into the elevator and keyed in the code for the third floor. As he stepped off, he could see into the glass-walled conference room. He watched as Seth pulled Samantha into his arms and lowered his head to kiss her. Her body froze and then it looked like she bit him. Seth could be a real asshole when he tried, but King knew him well enough to know Seth most likely knew he was on his way up. If he did, King would plant his fist in the fucker's face. If not, he would eviscerate the bastard.

Even though he knew this was Seth being Seth, he felt an overwhelming urge to smash Seth's pretty-boy face into the live-edge walnut conference table. If Seth hadn't grinned at him… if Samantha hadn't looked at him with the eyes of an angel, he might have let it pass. But neither of those things happened and King sent his fist into Seth's face with a satisfying crack of cartilage and spurting of blood.

"You're an asshole, Newcomb," he growled menacingly before turning to her and touching her cheek reverently. "Are you all right, baby?"

He reached out to her, praying she wouldn't recoil. She didn't, instead she came into his arms and kissed his bruised knuckles before covering his lips with hers and kissing him deeply.

"He didn't mean anything by it," she said. "I think he knew you were on your way and was just giving you shit."

"He has a death wish we don't like to talk about."

"Are either of you planning to help me? Both my nose and lip are bleeding. Your girl has razor sharp teeth, brother. I'd think twice before shoving my dick in her mouth."

King slapped him upside the head. "That's my woman you're talking about. Watch your mouth."

"Message received," said Seth. "I'm going to go see if I can fix my nose. If you've mangled it, either you or Fitz are paying the plastic surgeon." Seth left the room.

"Seriously, are you okay?"

"I am, but what the hell was that about? I didn't do anything to encourage him."

"I know that. Normally, I'd think he was either pushing my buttons just for fun or trying to make me admit how I feel about you, but he already knows that."

"That's nice. Like to clue me in?"

"I don't think you want to hear it."

Her body began to stiffen. "Don't worry about me, Coltraine. I'm a big girl. I can take care of myself. I wasn't expecting forever with you." King released her and leaned against the table as she turned away and began to pace. "I'm really grateful for all that you've done for me, especially in light of Jen being killed, and I've really enjoyed sleeping with you. But your life is here and mine is back in England. Once you've caught this guy, I won't hold anything you've said to me against you. We can go back to living our separate lives."

Seth walked back into the room, shaking his head slowly. "I only caught the tail end of that, but if at all possible, you might want to walk that back." He turned to Royce who had just come in with pizzas. "And you," Seth said pointing to Royce, "owe me a hundred bucks."

"What are you talking about?" asked Samantha.

"He kissed you…" started King.

"So that's why King broke your nose," interrupted Royce.

"As I started to say, Seth kissed you in some misguided attempt to make you admit your feelings."

"Only you walked in, misinterpreted what I was doing, and broke my nose."

"Why would Seth's kissing me clarify anything?"

"Did you like it?" Royce asked.

"Not particularly. I mean from a purely clinical or information gathering standpoint, I suppose it was okay, but it didn't move me the way Coltraine's kisses do."

Royce shook his head. "Like Seth said, you might want to walk that shit back. In case you missed it, the calmer he seems? The more pissed he is. Seth, ole son, why don't we leave a pizza up here for them and then head down to the conference room. I have a feeling it's about to get noisy."

"Why would it get noisy?" Samantha asked, clearly confused, as Seth and Royce left them alone.

She looked at him, then to Royce and Seth's retreating forms and back at him.

"Because one of two things is going to happen," said King calmly. "Either you're going to try and hold on to that aloof demeanor you just adopted, in which case I'm going to put you over my knee and turn your ass all kinds of red and painful, or you're going to strip naked, hand me your clothes, drop to your knees and apologize profusely. If it's the latter, I will magnanimously forgive you before tossing you over my shoulder and hauling you off to bed, where I will proceed to make you scream from the enormity of the pleasure I will inflict on you."

"You do know I am clueless as to what it is I'm supposed to have done, right?"

"Tell me, Samantha, did you really believe that claptrap you just spouted about going our separate ways and all?"

"That I don't want you to feel trapped? I mean, I know I'm an assignment and you've been very good to me, but it isn't like you signed on for forever."

"Didn't I?" he said, drawing the velvet pouch containing her collar from the front pocket of his jeans.

He opened the pouch and withdrew the collar he would expect her to wear until death did them part. Samantha gasped as he dangled it from his finger.

"You, Ms. Butler, are going nowhere. Am I clear about that?" She nodded. "Then make up your mind—my lap or your knees."

Samantha quietly but quickly removed her clothes, folding them neatly and putting them on the conference room table. She sank gracefully to her knees and into the submissive pose she knew he liked best.

"I'm very sorry, Sir…"

"It's Master from now on."

"Yes, Master. I'm very sorry that your poor sub failed to understand the situation or the depth of your feelings for her. It is a shortcoming I will endeavor to correct."

He circled her and watched her tremble, glad to recognize that it was arousal and not fear that provoked the response.

Standing behind her, he lifted her hair and removed the training collar before replacing it with the exquisite one he'd purchased earlier in the day. The sparkling diamonds, elegant pearls, and luminescent opal only enhanced her flawless skin. He walked back around in front of her and offered her his hand, which she took and rose to her feet.

"He was also pushing me. I've been concerned about adding to your stress and wasn't sure you wanted to hear how I felt. I see now that was a misjudgment on my part. You know the lifestyle is important to me. I've never even wanted to collar another woman until I met you. I'm sure there will be those who think the situation we're in made us do rash things. It didn't; it simply compressed time and made us realize what we had found. I love you, Samantha Butler. I can't imagine my life without you."

"I love you, too. I didn't want to and then I was so afraid that I loved you and you were only caring for me because you're a Dom…"

"Baby, not only have I never collared a sub before, but I've also never pulled her into my lap at every opportunity and fed her just so I can feel her breathe and know that she was safe and happy."

"In that case, can we take our pizza to bed and get to the part where you make me scream with pleasure?"

Leaning into her middle, he tossed her over his shoulder, grabbed the pizza, and took her back to their suite, locking them in and texting Royce that they were in for the night. He put the pizza on the table by the leather wingback by the window and then tossed her onto the bed.

"I think I can handle that."

He had no idea how it was all going to play out, but for tonight, he had Samantha Butler in his bed, she loved him, and was wearing his collar. What could possibly go wrong?

CHAPTER 19

SAMANTHA

It was an odd thing to love a man who loved you the way Kingston did. Sure, she wrote about it in books, but she'd always believed she was writing a fantasy. And yet here she was faced with that actual reality. She should be the happiest of women, and she was. But there were times she felt pangs of guilt over the fact that Jen had been killed because of her. It was fine to say that only the killer was responsible, but Samantha couldn't help thinking that if she'd never come here, never walked through the doors...

Smack! King's hand had connected with her ass as he'd walked toward their room with her slung over his shoulder much like a sack of grain.

"Wherever you just went in that pretty head of yours, don't," growled King as he'd keyed in the code.

"You don't know what I was thinking," she argued and earned another smack.

Who said the man couldn't multi-task?

"I may not know what you were thinking, but I know it wasn't good," he said as he tossed her on the bed.

"You don't know that, either."

"Yes, I do. You were all soft and yielding until something occurred to you and made your body tense up. Nothing that makes you tense, unless we're playing and you're anticipating something, is good, so stop."

"Tell me now, Samantha. This doesn't work if we aren't both honest with each other. That was part of Seth's point."

Samantha searched his face and all she saw was love and concern—not concern about their relationship and who they were to one another, but concern for her and her happiness.

"It just crossed my mind that maybe if I hadn't come into the club the other day…"

King groaned. "…that Jen might be alive. We've done this, baby. She could have been killed going home that night, or hit by a bus crossing the street or if she was going sailing with friends—she could have fallen in and drowned."

"But she didn't. She went to get my things out of the locker and whoever my stalker is killed her. I know you're going to say we don't really know that for certain…" Her words trailed off as she saw his shoulders sink and his body sort of deflate. "What?"

"I wasn't going to tell you and for that I apologize. I shouldn't have tried to keep it from you. You're the client; you have a right to know. But more than that, you're my lover and my woman and if it concerns you, I sure as fuck shouldn't be keeping secrets."

He reached into his pocket and made a call to Royce, tossing her his shirt to put on. "You, Seth, and your pizzas should come join us in the war room. I have news. I was going to wait until tomorrow, but I need to tell Samantha and it doesn't make sense for me not to tell you all at once. Grab some beers." He kissed her. "I'm sorry. Let's go sit down and we'll all talk."

"Is it bad?"

"Yes, but we're better for the knowing."

King took her hand and went to lead her back, but she resisted, digging in her heels. He stopped and looked at her—his expression heartbreaking.

"I love you. I don't care what you did or didn't do or tell me. I know that whatever it was, you did it for me. I just wanted you to know that."

He smiled. "And here I thought I'd only fallen in love with you for your sexy body, dirty mind, and perverted nature."

"Well, lover," she said moving past him and taking the pizza, "I wouldn't discount that, but they don't have to be the only reasons."

He chuckled and fell in behind her. Seth and Royce were just getting off the elevator as Samantha and King came around the corner of King's office.

"There's not going to be any more blood tonight, is there?" said Seth cheekily.

"I'm not willing to commit to that," said King. "The day is still young."

"Geeze, what's wrong with you," Seth said to Samantha, "Usually, he's in a much better mood when he's been laid by you."

This time it was Royce who hit Seth upside the head. "You dumb shit. He's been busy with other things. The collar is gorgeous, Samantha. King is a lucky bastard." He started into the war room ahead of everyone, stopping in the doorway and turning back to look between them. "You almost make me want to start believing in true love."

Pizzas and beer open and ready to be consumed, King took control of the remote. Samantha often-times found it amusing to watch the three of them vying for control of the device.

"I had Sully put a filter on Samantha's emails…"

"You what?" she huffed.

"I was trying to keep you away from any of the emails that were becoming more threatening," he held up his hands in surrender, "in the vain belief you would be safer. And yes, I know how stupid that was." He reached over and took her hand, bringing it to his lips to kiss.

"I take it Sully intercepted one?" asked Royce.

"Not just one—several," said King, clicking the remote so that several emails popped up on the big screen. "The unsub now holds Samantha responsible not only for writing dirty books and propagating sin, but for Jen's death. According to Jen's killer, Samantha is responsible for her death."

"That is bullshit," snarled Samantha. "Some crackpot doesn't like what I write, so instead of just not reading my books, he makes me a target and kills someone because it wasn't me?"

"Basically, that's the logic," said King. "I didn't put all of the emails up on the screen."

"You mean there's more?" asked Seth.

"My guess is they get worse," said Royce. "King has displayed them in order. What I find fascinating is they become more violent and more frequent."

King inclined his head in recognition that Royce's assumption was right. "Part of what is making the unsub angrier is that Sully has a program that can keep the recipient from knowing that the email was opened. All of the emails contained a kind of hidden tracker, so the stalker knew if and when the emails weren't open. Now he thinks Samantha is ignoring him."

"So, you're egging him on," said Samantha, trying to understand.

"Yes, but to a purpose. Sully wanted to see if you ignoring him would make him escalate, which it did. I would never have approved this if we hadn't had you under lock and key."

"Or, as we like to say in the business, under close cover," quipped Seth.

"Would you like him to break the rest of your face?" asked Royce in a droll tone.

"As I said, the day is still young," said King with more menace than she hoped he actually meant.

"The emails that aren't on the screen are pretty lurid and violent. I'd prefer you not see them," commented King in a neutral tone.

Taking his hand, she squeezed reassuringly. "I promise I won't let them frighten me, but I might see them in a different light or be able to give them added meaning."

"How so?" asked King.

"Remember how you noted the phrase the stalker used in several of the emails?" He nodded. "I write dialogue all day long—dialogue that this bastard has read, my guess is, repeatedly. I might spot something there that the three of you or even Sully doesn't."

"I'm sure he's putting it through one of his programs…"

"Maybe, but maybe he hasn't gotten that far…"

King dropped down the second screen and put up the latest emails.

"The first thing, which I'm sure all of you and Sully can see, is that the emails become more emphatic, less rational." She stood up, walking towards the screen and then stopped, looking around. "Sorry, I tend to think out loud because usually there's no one around. And I tend to pace when I'm irritated or upset."

"She also bites," quipped Seth.

King growled at Seth and then turned back to her. "Go on, Samantha, you're on a roll."

"Okay. At first the unsub is making vague threats and the whole 'he knows who I am' thing."

"Duh, you don't have a pen name," smirked Seth.

"But I don't think that's what he means," said King, leaning forward.

Samantha bobbed her head. "Exactly. This cretin —and I get to use words like that because I'm a writer —thinks he knows everything about me based on what he's read. I don't think all of the anger is because of what I write or that I didn't open these last emails. I'm not acting the way he thinks I should."

"You've thrown him a curve ball. He's starting to come unwound because he doesn't know how you'll react."

He held out his hand to her, glad to see her take it and allow herself to be settled in his lap. He'd once wondered about Fitz's constant wanting to have the woman he was crazy in love and lust with near. King understood it now. His cock may want nothing more than to spend the rest of its existence enveloped by her warm, wet heat, but there was also a part of her that soothed him and helped him to think more clearly.

"I don't know that this is much about you at all," said Royce.

"What do you mean?" asked King.

"The unsub is becoming more unhinged, but now he's blaming Samantha for all the things that are wrong in his life. Like things are becoming unraveled and he's holding her responsible."

"One more little piece of the puzzle, Sully has tracked down the geographical location for the source —Chicago. Sweetheart, could the unsub have found some way to herd you toward Chicago?"

"I wouldn't think so and it doesn't make sense. The emails began to really escalate after I was already here."

"True. I had breakfast this morning with Matt Dillon…"

"That cop?" sniffed Samantha disdainfully.

"He's not a bad sort."

"And he spotted me tailing him within a couple of blocks of Elmo's," added Royce.

"In any event," said King, "he wanted to meet with me. He said he and Moore are feeling pressure from up the chain of command to let Samantha's case and Jen's murder slowly sink to the bottom of the heap to be ignored."

Seth tipped his chair forward, all of his relaxed

body posture gone. "Are you suggesting this whack job is someone with the police department?"

"That's the only conclusion I can come to," said King.

"Flushing him out is going to be tricky," said Royce.

"Tricky, but not impossible. Less so with Dillon's help."

"How do you figure?" asked Samantha.

"Dillon is going to become a member of the club. It gives him a reason to be here so we can meet and exchange information."

"You think he can help us?" asked Seth.

King shrugged. "If nothing else, he can tell us of any pressure that's being applied."

"So, he agrees that someone is exerting undue influence on the brass."

"He does, although I'm not sure he's right," King said, thoughtfully.

"You think it's somebody within the department itself," said Royce.

King nodded. "That makes the most sense. If one of the top cops has killed someone, they're going to want to make sure that the investigation into Jen's death never comes close to them."

"Anybody in the upper brass joining the club?" asked Samantha.

"The chief of detectives. Married but joining as a single."

Samantha frowned. "Is that allowed?"

"We're not the morality police. In some ways, if one person is so inclined and the other isn't it can create a lot of friction. Sometimes the one who joins is actually trying to save his marriage."

"I don't think that would work for me," said Samantha.

"I didn't say it worked; I've just known more than one person whose partner can't provide what they need and so they turn to the club."

They ate in thoughtful silence. She thought about how comfortable she'd become in the short amount of time she'd known them. Granted, the case had compressed time, but still she knew these were men she would know for the rest of her life. Sighing, she leaned back against King's chest before bolting upright.

"Samantha?"

"I have a great idea, but you're not going to like it. Seth? Royce? I need you to back me."

"That's not the way it works, Samantha. A smart man," Royce said looking at Seth, "never comes between a Dom and his sub, even when he's trying to make a point."

"He wouldn't have listened," said Seth, defending himself.

King sighed. "I'm really not going to like this."

"Like what?" asked Seth.

"Samantha is about to suggest that she put herself

up as bait to lure out the unsub, aren't you sweetheart?"

"Do you have a better idea?"

She grinned in triumph because she knew her idea was solid. They were going to have to provoke the unsub into coming out from the shadows and what better place to do so than a location where they controlled all of the components of the sting, except the stalker himself.

CHAPTER 20

Two hours later they had a rough idea of how they could pull off the op and keep Samantha safe at the same time. Fitz and JJ had planned to attend the gala and perhaps stick around for the grand opening, but now Sawyer and Rhiannon, as well as Nigel and Olivia would be there as well. Rhiannon would be there mostly because they could conceal her up in the rafters with her sniper rifle.

Once he had Samantha back in their room, King locked the door. Royce and Seth would do another sweep after they finished finalizing the plans.

"Please don't be angry with me," she whispered apologetically.

"I'm not. I don't like you being put at risk, but I also don't think there's a way to get around it. This guy is building up and he's going to need another way to vent his fury. You heard Dillon when we talked to him. The department's shrink thinks that's really why he killed Jen. The unsub needed a way to express what was boiling inside him and she was a convenient target. I agree that even if it had been you, the unsub would have just picked someone else on whom to focus his rage."

"I liked her," Samantha said.

"So did I. The reason she joined us and pushed to be trained to work with Cerberus was because she wanted her life to mean something. She told Seth she didn't just want to die an old woman in her bed regretting all the things she hadn't done. I think she would have liked knowing her death brought a psycho to justice."

"How do you figure that?"

"If she hadn't been murdered, the unsub would never have needed to try and quash the investigation. I know everyone else seems to think that somehow your stalker lured you here, but I disagree. It was only after you arrived, inadvertently getting closer to the unsub, that he lost control and lashed out. The last thing he wanted was you here in Chicago."

"Will you do me a favor?"

"If I can."

"Could you just be my Dom tonight? Could you just make love to me, make me scream your name, and make me forget all of the ugliness so I can sleep basking in your love?"

"Yes, baby, I can do that," he crooned, smiling.

Swinging her back up in his arms he carried her to their bed and stretched her out in it, her arms over her head. He sat on the edge, leaning over her and inhaling deeply. He loved the coconutty smell of the shampoo she used, and the fresh cucumber smell from her soap, but it was the sweet, tangy scent of her arousal that he breathed in like a magical elixir he couldn't live without.

He marveled at how she had gone from someone he didn't even know existed to the single most important thing in his life. She was his center; the best part of himself resided with her. He thanked the god or gods or whatever it was that controlled the universe for bringing her into his life and for allowing her to feel the same way about him.

She brought her hands down to caress him. He caught her wrists with one hand to put them back where he wanted them as he snapped his hand against her pussy.

"They stay where I put them," he snarled. He was feeling way too much—adrenaline, arousal, anticipation, apprehension—to not have control. Maybe if he could control her, he could control himself and everything around them.

He covered her mouth with his, kissing her deeply before trailing his kisses down her jaw to her throat and onward to the valley between her breasts. He leaned over, sucking her stiff nipple into his mouth, swirling his tongue around it before biting down gently and making her hiss.

"I hate, and yet love, when you do that to me."

"That's the idea," he rumbled deeply. "I mean to light you up so that when I thrust inside you, you go off like a rocket."

He began making good on his threat: licking, sucking, and nipping his way down her body with his mouth. His hands played their own game: stroking, pinching, tugging, and smacking her sex, her thighs, and her backside. He moved swiftly and surely but took his time in doing so, waiting for her response.

"You are driving me crazy."

"Good thing it's not a long road," he chortled as he moved down her body, spreading her thighs and whispering kisses all along over her sex.

Her desire and need kicked into overdrive. He licked the opening to her core. She wasn't just wet; she was soaked and squirming beneath him. The scent of her arousal was driving him out of his mind. A primitive, feral version of himself was beginning to take over. The caveman wanted his mate and meant to have her screaming and writhing beneath him.

Sliding his upper arms under her legs, he gave her slit another lick before latching his mouth to her and beginning to feast. Over and over he speared her with his tongue, flattening it out inside her so he could lap up her honey. His tongue and mouth were covered in her, and nothing had ever tasted better.

He was able to reach her clit with his hand and played with her swollen nub, pressing down on it as he drove deep with his tongue. Her body arched up and she called his name as she came in a powerful climax that left her trembling in its aftermath. He stroked her body and kissed it in acknowledgement that he was there and to ready her for his possession.

King gently let her thighs relax on the bed as he began to move up her body. "Do you have any idea how much I love and need you?" He guided her legs up so that they were wrapped around him.

Samantha smiled, all too willing to do what he asked in the afterglow of her orgasm and because she knew there was more to come. He slid his cock back and forth in her natural lubrication. Looking deep into her eyes, he thrust up into her, impaling her completely, groaning in exultation as he did so.

King hissed, drawing back until he was almost completely out of her before driving back in. He kissed her as he began to establish his rhythm. He wanted to just revel in her body and enjoy not just the sex, but the intimacy they shared. Every sigh, every caress, every pulse within her core spoke to him and reiterated that she was his other half—the best part of him.

When he felt her body trembling in anticipation, he turned loose his control. It was only with Samantha that he could let go and set the savage beast inside him free. Samantha cried out as her pussy spasmed up and down his hard length, pushing him over into his own orgasm as he filled her with his seed.

It seemed to take forever for him to empty his balls as he ground against her. The sheer ecstasy of the way her pussy milked his dick was pleasure personified. He collapsed on top of her, resting his head next to hers.

"God, I love you," he whispered, rolling off her but holding her close so that she ended up half on top of him. "I'll get him, Samantha. No one will take you from me."

She kissed his neck. "I know that, King. I believe in you."

He held her close as she drifted into a peaceful sleep.

I don't know who you are motherfucker, but come party time, your ass is mine.

Samantha

A few days later, Samantha awoke nestled against King's strength. She groaned inwardly. The invitation-only gala was tonight. Being with King had proved to her that her libido could be used for other things than to write steamy romance novels. It had also shown her how very much she liked snuggling and to care for and be cared about. King's arms tightened around her, and he buried his face in her hair.

"No," he growled softly.

"What do you mean no? I haven't asked or done anything."

"I know, but you will. You're going to remind me of all the things we need to get done before the gala this evening. Once again, while I may agree this is likely the best plan, I don't have to like it. You should know that if at any point I think your safety is compromised, I can and will pull the plug."

"Cerberus…"

"Doesn't have a say. I know Fitz. If I tell him, you're out—you're out. He once left JJ cuffed to a headboard in a safehouse to keep her safe. Trust me, I won't have any trouble convincing Fitz this is a bad idea and I need to get you out of here to ensure your safety."

Samantha rolled her eyes and felt King's hand snap against her ass.

"What was that for?" she asked.

"I heard you rolling your eyes."

Despite her annoyance, she couldn't help but laugh. He really was impossible. He was also wonderful.

There was a soft knock on the door. King reached over her to hit the speaker for the intercom.

"Yeah?"

"Good morning to you too, sunshine. You and your lady better get dressed. The gang from London just landed. They're headed into the office."

They got up and shared a shower. Even when he didn't fuck her there, there was a burgeoning intimacy that seemed to grow each day. They no longer recognized or even noticed one another's personal space. Once they were dressed, they headed out to the war room.

One look at Seth's face and she knew something had happened. Royce and King had great poker faces. They were both hard to read, but Seth's face was an open book.

"What's happened?" King asked as he fixed two mugs of coffee and then sank into his usual chair, pulling her into his lap.

"That resort Adam and Chelsea went to over the holidays? They went back as guests of the owners… and got snowed in. They won't be with us tonight."

"What else?" asked King.

"There's been another email. The guy is losing it and Fitz is already talking about getting Samantha out of here."

Before she could speak, King shook his head. "That won't work. If he knows about the party, he'll come anyway and then head after her. If he's just fixated on her, and the last couple of messages indicated that he now wants to take out all of us, he'll go after her anyway. Let's see it."

Seth, flipped it up onto the big screen:

Butler, you whore. You think you can hide from me, but you can't. I know you're at Chicago's newest den of iniquity.

All of your perversions and friends are known to me. You're all whores and perverts.

I am here. I am powerful. I am watching.

You and your friends will die tonight.

"Much as I hate to admit it," said King. "Samantha is right. We need to draw this guy out and take him down. I think I speak for Fitz when I say one way or another it ends tonight. Either we can arrest him and hand him over to Dillon, or we end him, permanently."

For the first time since she'd met King, she was afraid. As long as she'd been bundled up here in their building, she'd felt invulnerable. The danger and menace had seemed distant.

It wasn't distant any longer. The people he was threatening were her friends. Her lover.

"He must sense we're closing in on him," said King. "The last time I talked to Dillon he said Moore had pretty much checked out. The pressure from above has a lot of detectives and support people saying to let it go."

Royce chuckled. "Dudley Do-Right will never do that. The guy is a freaking boy scout, but I kind of like him. Has he thought what this might cost him career-wise?"

"I think so," said King. "I don't think he cares. But I talked to Fitz. If they fire his ass, we're going to offer him a job. He's green and he has no black ops experience, but we can train him. You can't train a sense of right or justice. We'll make sure he's okay."

He stroked her back and Samantha knew the last part had been for her benefit.

"He really seems to have amped up his rhetoric," said Seth. "Now it's not just Samantha, it's all of us perverts and whores."

"And there's no telling if he'll stop if he gets us," added Royce.

"I think he's reacting to the fact that he can't get to me, and he can't get Dillon to back off. I think Dillon needs to be here with us. With Moore not having his back, he's really vulnerable."

"Not to worry, baby, we've got him covered. Now all we have to do is wait for the team and flush this sucker out."

"Then what?" she asked.

He clucked his tongue at her. "Tsk. Tsk. You're supposed to be the romance writer. You should know this. We catch the bad guy, save the damsel in distress, and live happily ever after."

Samantha stared at him and felt her lips curling up in a smile. Not so long ago she wouldn't have believed him. Now, if they could just survive the night, she might very well get her fairytale ending.

CHAPTER 21

They'd spent the entire day going over plans, looking for weaknesses, and walking the club. Samantha had been taking mental notes so that the next time she wanted to write a scene about how a group set up to take down a bad guy, she'd be able to inject some realism into it. She loved writing about romance with heroic alpha males and about how love conquers all, but she wanted the romance—the idyllic romantic fantasy—to be set in realism so that she could sweep her readers away on an adventure.

She was a member of Baker Street and so had met and heard a lot of the stories about the three couples who would be joining them: Fitz and JJ, Nigel and Olivia, and Sawyer and Rhiannon. Each had been through their own trials, and each had emerged victorious and madly in love. Samantha had worried that if King pulled her into his lap, she'd feel awkward, but seeing JJ, Olivia and Rhiannon doing the same had put her at ease.

Samantha was finishing up her hair, getting ready to go down to the club alongside Rhiannon, who had appointed herself Samantha's bodyguard unless one of the 'boys,' as she called them, could be right beside her. Once they were dressed in fet wear and King was back at her side, Rhiannon would work her way up into the rafters. Rafters where she had hidden three different sniper rifles at various points where she could target the entire dungeon.

King came up behind her, wrapping one arm around her waist and dropping a kiss on her shoulder. "You don't have to do this if you don't want to."

"I do. The stalker may have started out after me, but he killed Jen and now he's threatened all of you. There's no way I let you walk into this alone, without me."

He locked gazes with her in the mirror, a soft smile lighting his eyes. "Did you miss the people we spent the day with? I'd hardly be alone. Fitz, Nigel, and Sawyer all want you to get cold feet."

"Why?"

"Because then they can convince JJ, Olivia, and Rhiannon to stand down. The argument would be if you aren't going, neither are JJ and Olivia, and Rhiannon would be assigned to protect you—most likely on a transatlantic flight back to London."

Samantha turned in his arms. "Think that

through—the four of us alone, deciding we'll take this sucker down without any of you."

"That's what I told them would happen."

"I hope what they brought for me from Baker Street looks all right. I've always abided by the rules, but I've honestly never had one of those beautiful corsets the other girls wear."

"Not to worry. I've taken care of your attire for the evening. If you want, just pull on one of my sweaters and a pair of leggings for now. I put your things for this evening in your locker for you earlier, and I want you to put on everything that's in the bag. Understand?"

"What did you buy?"

"Never you mind. But I mean it. I know exactly what I left for you and if you're not wearing all of it, I'll spank you so hard you won't sit for a week."

Samantha leaned back and searched his face, which was a curious mix of emotions. He was dead-ass serious, and yet his eyes danced with merriment and joy. She took King's suggestion and pulled on one of his sweaters and a pair of leggings. King was dressed in his outfit for the night: well-fitted leathers with a button up fly as well as a matching leather vest, no shirt, and boots. He was every inch the alpha male Dom of her and so many of her readers' dreams.

Once inside the submissives' salon, Samantha found her locker, which was actually more of a small armoire, with her name on it.

"Fitz said King made some people work overtime so that your locker was ready," said JJ with a knowing smile. "I take it he's chosen your outfit for the night and left it for you?"

"So I'm told. Should I be worried?"

"That depends. What did he say?"

"That he'd chosen everything I was to wear, and I was to put all of it on. So hopefully if there's a corset, one of you can help me with it."

"If?" laughed Olivia. "*If* there's a corset? My dear Samantha, where the men of Cerberus are concerned, there's *always* a corset."

Even though she'd known these women for a couple of years, she felt she'd grown so much closer to them. Grinning, she opened the locker and removed the bag from Speak Easy. The silhouette of a vintage corset on the front of the bag left little doubt about what it contained.

Samantha reached in and pulled out a beautiful, delicate scrap of silk and lace material that she imagined was supposed to pass for panties.

"Do they not know how uncomfortable those things are?" snorted Rhiannon. "They barely cover anything and then it's like having a piece of dental floss drawn up between your butt cheeks."

"I've pointed that out to Nigel, who said if I didn't like a thong I could do without."

They all laughed as Samantha stripped out of her

leggings and wriggled into the skimpy garment. "I'm not sure there's much difference."

She reached into the bag and pulled out the matching leather corset with the hand embroidery. There was a collective gasp.

"That is stunning," said Rhiannon. "We may have to hit up that new casino in Miami before we go home. Easy Street I think they call it."

Samantha pulled King's sweater over her head and shimmied into the corset. Stepping over to the row of bars set into the wall for subs to hang onto while someone tightened their corset, Samantha breathed in and allowed JJ to lace her up. The proprietress of Baker Street had a deft hand with laces and in no time at all, Samantha's new corset had not only made the best of her figure, with her boobs looking like they were in danger of falling out, but she was actually comfortable.

"Nobody laces a corset like JJ. You look great and you can actually breathe," said Olivia. "I like these bars, JJ. We should get these installed at Baker Street."

"Fitz and I are negotiating about that. I want them in the submissives' salon like here. He wants them just outside so the Doms can do the lacing."

"Ladies, no corsets for me tonight… at least not until we catch this bastard. God, I want him to do something so I can just drop him," said Rhiannon. "You going to be all right until you rejoin the men?" The other women nodded. "Right then. I'm going up.

I'll see you all later." She left through a back entrance that led to a maze of back halls that led up to the roof's interior structure.

"And Seth calls me bloodthirsty," quipped Samantha, who spun around when she heard Olivia gasp.

"What's wrong?" demanded JJ.

"Nothing. I think I found the item in the bag King was the most insistent you put on."

"I already have his collar," said Samantha walking toward her.

"Yes, and he put something in your bag I think will match," said Olivia holding up a velvet ring box.

Samantha stopped and looked at her as if she were holding a venomous snake. She started to back away, shaking her head. JJ's hand just below her shoulder blades propelled her forward.

"He never said anything," stammered Samantha.

"Cheeky bastard. Want me to shove it in his face and tell him to man up?" asked JJ.

"Are you crazy?" replied Samantha. She snatched the box from Olivia's hand. "I wouldn't want to disobey or disappoint my master."

She knew it was a ring. It had to be a ring. What if it wasn't a ring?

Tentatively, as if the box might actually contain a snake—albeit a very tiny one, Samantha opened the box and was absolutely gobsmacked. She was a writer. She was supposed to be good with words, but her vocabulary failed her.

It was most definitely a ring… her ring. It wasn't a snake or any other reptile. Instead, it was a large white opal surrounded by seed pearls and diamonds—just like her choker— and it was stunning.

"I'd hand it to him and tell him he can either get down on one knee and propose like a proper gentleman or the deal's off," said JJ.

"No way. This is my ring and I'm keeping it," said Samantha as she placed the ring on her finger. "It's gorgeous."

"That's true. I see Coltraine is playing the 'let's see if I can one up the rest of them' game. Honestly, men can be such little boys," said Olivia.

"As long as they're hung like horses, who gives a damn?" quipped JJ.

"Could you ladies do me a favor and head on out. I want a minute to compose myself, so I don't go out there crying my eyes out and ruining my mascara."

"The boys were adamant you weren't to be left alone," said Olivia.

"What could happen? There's security all over the place. No one is allowed in the salon tonight unless accompanied on a tour. It's just all happened so fast."

"Little Miss Goody Two Shoes," teased JJ.

"That's Lady Goody Two Shoes to you," responded Olivia.

"You take all the time you need," said JJ. "It'll be payback for just leaving the damn thing in your bag. And Olivia's right—that ring ranks right up there with the rest of them, although I must say mine is best. We'll see you out there. Come along, Olivia, don't be such a goose."

"Fine, but I want it noted for the record I was not a part of this."

Samantha walked over to the full-length mirror. She felt like Cinderella about to go to the ball—only Cinderella had a ball gown and glass slippers. Samantha had a leather corset, matching thong, and matching ring and collar. All in all, she much preferred what she had. Besides, Prince Charming had always seemed so dull.

She looked around. She knew this club and lifestyle would always be a part of them, but their lives would also include lazy Sunday mornings where they only got out of bed to fix something to eat, a loft in the city with a private balcony overlooking the lake where she could sit naked in King's lap having coffee, and long lovemaking sessions where he made her give up far more orgasms than she thought she had to give.

There were no two ways about it, she was madly, irrevocably in love with Kingston Coltraine. He'd swept her off her feet, given her no choice, and had made all of her secret dreams come true.

A sound from behind her caught her attention. JJ or Olivia must have forgotten something. When she turned around it wasn't either of them. Instead, it was a tall, elegantly dressed woman with a short, textured pixie haircut. She recognized her as the deputy chief of police.

"I'm sorry, the salon is off-limits this evening. Can I show you back to the lounge?"

The woman said nothing and just stared at her. The growing silence was making Samantha more uncomfortable by the minute.

"Deputy Chief Meadows," started Samantha, hoping her knowledge of who the woman was might deter whatever she was planning.

"You couldn't leave well-enough alone, could you?" the woman asked in a cold, flat voice, pulling a small gun with a suppressor out of her purse. "I thought you would stay in London. I thought after I killed that girl you would go back, maybe even stop writing your filth. But no, you had to stay."

"You?"

The woman chuckled. "Why not me? Because I'm a woman? My husband read that book where you had the male submissive, he thought we should try that. It was disgusting. He's on the City Council for god's sake, and he wants me to put his cock and balls in some kind of cage? He wanted to call me mistress? Why do I always have to carry the burden? Why couldn't he just be normal? I found out he joined some club out in San Francisco so he could pay hookers to abuse him."

"Torch Light? They don't allow paid sex workers, and D/s isn't just about sex."

The chuckle became a brutal laugh. "You just keep telling yourself that. I'll bet that handsome hulk who's been protecting you has his way with you whenever he wants." Samantha nodded. She had to stall for time. "Disgusting." She waved the gun towards the back.

"There's nothing back there but showers."

The deputy chief, who was now standing within striking distance, backhanded her with the gun. "You stupid cow. Don't you think I studied the building plans? You and I are leaving."

Samantha backed away. To leave Club Southside would mean her death and she had no intention of dying before she'd had a long and full life with King.

The last words he'd said to her were a warning to not be alone, not even in the bathroom. She was to have someone with her at all times. And what had she done? She'd shooed everyone out and was now facing down a madwoman.

King was going to be pissed.

CHAPTER 22

KING

He alternated between mingling with guests and waiting in the lounge as long as he could stand it. What if the ring had been too much? What if she hadn't thought leaving it in the bag was sweet and endearing? What if she was pissed? Well, the last he could handle easily enough and they could talk through the other two… couldn't they? He tossed back the last of his scotch.

"Something on your mind, lad?" asked Fitzwallace.

The former SAS officer was probably the only one who could call any of the men who made up Cerberus 'lad' and not either get his teeth knocked out or be laughed out of the club. The fact was, Fitz had hand-picked each and every member of the team. They comprised the best of the best. There wasn't a black-ops, elite fighting force that was their equal. But right now, King was worried that he had misplayed this whole proposal thing.

"No. I just want to check on Samantha."

"You afraid she's going to give you trouble about the ring?"

King looked at Fitz sharply. "How'd you know?"

The Scotsman chuckled. "I've known you to walk into overwhelming odds without batting an eye. You're one of the bravest men I know. The only thing that would have you this concerned was if you were planning to put a ring on her finger. Take it from me, lad, don't ask; tell."

King smiled. "Actually, I just left it with her corset and thong and told her I expected her to have everything in the bag on when she came out."

Fitz laughed. "That's the way to do it. Give her a minute. Have another drink."

He was just about to do so when Olivia and JJ joined them in the lounge. He tapped his communication device. "Rhiannon?"

"Yep. Ready and waiting."

"Fuck," King swore. "Then who's with Samantha?"

He bolted from the lounge, Seth and Royce hot on his heels. In his ear, he could hear Fitzwallace barking orders to quietly gather their guests and get them to safety. All those not involved in that were to head toward the submissives' salon.

Rhiannon would have to stay up in the rafters where she could cover more of the club. Sawyer would join her so there would be two top shooters overseeing everyone's safety.

King burst through the door into the salon. There was no one there. They couldn't have gotten out the front and no one but Cerberus knew about the hidden exit. No one, except someone who'd seen the building plans. They ended their search at the hidden exit.

Why had he left her alone? Why hadn't he made her change upstairs and then come down and stay with him? Why? They'd been so smug that they were the best and no one could foil their plans. No one but a stubborn romance novelist and a bunch of arrogant black ops people.

They drew their guns and charged into the alley. There was no one. No sound. Nothing. If Samantha had been taken out of the building by this entrance, she was gone.

They moved back towards the front to regroup and figure this out. They had to figure this out. He would not lose Samantha to a madman. King hadn't quite rounded the corner when Dillon collided with him.

He grabbed the young detective by the lapels. "Who has access to the building plans?"

"That's what I was just coming to tell you. Deputy Chief Meadows requested them. Her husband's having a meltdown. He's a submissive and his wife is pissed. It's not a man, King— the unsub is the deputy chief."

"Fuck me. Where would she take Samantha? We have to find her."

King, who it had always been said had ice in his veins, tamped down all his fear for the woman he loved more than life itself and forced himself to think like an operative. He turned to look back down the alley. The deputy chief had to be smart enough not to come around the front, and her car had a driver. That meant they were still on foot.

"Spread out. Dillon, go back around and tell Fitz. Tell him Seth is headed down the alley. Royce and I are going up. Royce, head to the roof of Cerberus. I'll take the building across the alley. They can't have been that long. The deputy chief will probably be in heels and Samantha will be in bare feet."

Royce ran towards the Cerberus building. King headed to the building across the alley and began to climb the fire escape. It wasn't likely the stalker would go back into Cerberus and they were nowhere to be seen on the street. That meant they had to have gone up and the building next door would be far easier to get to the roof than the building that housed Cerberus and Club Southside. They'd designed it that way. If he'd failed her... if he was too late... if she was dead, he'd just lie down beside her and die as well. When he pulled the fire escape down, it made a lot of noise, but once he was on his way up, he became a silent predator. He could only hope that the deputy chief was too involved in taking Samantha and the sounds of the city had at least muffled his pursuit.

Could the deputy chief force Samantha up the fire escape? Doubtful. They couldn't have gone back into the Cerberus building. What was the deputy chief planning? She could shoot Samantha or, more likely, if they were headed for the roof, she could force Samantha over the edge. The odds of surviving a fall from the top of the five-story building weren't good. But if they'd gone inside to get to the roof, he could be waiting for them.

Samantha

Samantha had tried to move as slowly as she could to give King and the rest of Cerberus time to realize she was in trouble.

"Why?" she asked again.

"Because you and your kind are a disgrace. I can't believe how many people—good, decent people—want to join this place. Women being paraded around practically nude, kneeling to men who are no better than they are. People being tied up, tied to equipment and beaten. The thought of it makes me sick. And all around you can smell the women dripping with arousal. Charles talked me into going to the one in

San Francisco. It was a freak show. I couldn't get out of there fast enough."

"But no one is forcing you. Why do you care?"

"Aren't they? You and all the other authors like you have made this kind of behavior acceptable—mainstream, even. Well not in my city."

"Club Southside is not the first lifestyle club in Chicago, just the newest and best."

"And once I get this one closed down, I'll start on the rest."

For an older woman, the deputy chief was incredibly strong. As she dragged Samantha to the Cerberus' hidden emergency exit, she thrust open the door and the cold, windy Chicago night assaulted them both. The deputy chief dragged her across the alley and then began forcing her up to and then onto the roof, seemingly oblivious to the cold.

Samantha knew from their discussion of contingencies this afternoon that by now, they had to know she was missing and so all of the guests would have been taken outside while a team of Cerberus operatives swept the building. Where was King? He always said he could feel her presence. If she screamed, would he hear her?

"Don't. You'll be dead before so much as a sound escapes those painted lips of yours."

The deputy chief dragged her toward the side of the building, avoiding air conditioning units and vents.

"You can't think you'll get away with this," started Samantha.

"Can't I?" Samantha saw a body propped up against the wall that surrounded the roof. The man moaned. It was Detective Moore. "He's been bad mouthing you and your books and your lifestyle since before Cerberus came to town. His wife is in hospice and not expected to see the sunrise. In his grief that a good woman like her was dying while you wrote your filth and lived your perversion, he broke, and he dragged you up here, throwing you off the roof before killing himself. You're not the only one with a flair for the dramatic."

"You won't get away with it. Your plot's a little weak."

"But I will. I'll either get away cleanly after having an argument with my husband and going home or I'll have heroically followed him up here but tragically failed to save either of you."

Samantha could have written a better version of that story, but all in all, it would probably hold up and the deputy chief might get away with it. Unless… behind the deputy chief, a shadow moved. She would have to tell King he was right; she had felt his presence a moment before she saw the darkness move. He moved with stealth and power. The deputy chief didn't know it, but the odds of this working out the way she wanted had just turned against her.

"None of those so-called Doms care about you idiots. No one is coming for you."

Samantha knew she was wrong; she couldn't really see King but could make out a shadow moving in the darkness, coming closer with each passing moment.

"You're wrong." She held up her hand. "King gave me this ring. We're getting married and we're going to live happily ever after despite what you think."

"I'd listen to her, deputy chief. I'll make you a deal. You walk away from Samantha, and I'll give you a head start to get away," said King as he stepped outside the only pool of light.

The deputy chief spun toward the sound, trying to spot King in the darkness. She fired two shots in his general direction and Samantha broke away from her, diving for cover behind one of the large metal vents.

The deputy chief fired again into empty space. The sound of King's Glock was not muffled in the least and two shots rang out in the dark. The deputy chief crumbled to the ground, dead before she hit the floor of the roof.

Samantha leapt to her feet and was pulled into King's strong embrace. "I've got you, baby. I've got you." He tapped his communication device. "Fitz, we need a bus. Detective Moore has been injured. I'm not sure how badly. I have Samantha and the deputy chief is dead."

The next few hours were a cacophony of sirens,

lights and cops and other officials running around a little bit like chickens with their heads cut off. Detective Moore was airlifted from the roof and flown to the same hospital where his wife lay dying, but not before giving a statement describing just what had happened and exonerating King.

Detective Dillon helped gather the Cerberus group back in their building and then dispersed the crowd of guests.

"There goes any hope of the club being run at a profit," said King as he sank down into one of the lounge chairs, pulling Samantha into his lap and bringing a tumbler of scotch to his lips.

"Don't be so certain, lad," said Fitz with a gleam in his eye. "While we had a slightly less dramatic event at Baker Street, it hit the papers, and membership applications soared. As long as the good guys come out on top—which is where every Dom wants to be—we'll be fine."

Without saying a word, King pulled the ring from Samantha's finger, then stood up and set her on her feet. "I was informed by Mrs. Fitzwallace that just leaving you the ring was a cowardly, bullshit way to ask you to marry me. If I could stand the thought of your ring not being on your finger, I'd arrange for some over-the-top, insanely creative way to do this, but you're the creative one."

King dropped to his knee and took her hand in his. "I love you, Samantha Butler, with every fiber of my being, and if you agree to be my wife, I'll make sure you know that every single day."

Tears welled in her eyes. She was pretty damn sure that Kingston Coltraine had never gotten on his knees for anyone. He loved her. If he wanted to get married that was fine, and if he didn't that would have been fine, as well… but she did love the ring.

"You gave me that ring. It's mine. Give it back."

"Do not," growled Fitzwallace, "I repeat do not give her that ring until she gets down on her knees and apologizes to you for disobeying you, almost getting herself killed, and not giving you a proper answer."

King stood up and pulled her into his arms. "He has a point. You did disobey me, which almost got you killed, but I'll make you a one-time deal. You say 'yes, Master, I'll marry you,' and I'll let the first two slide."

"Yes, Master, I'll marry you," agreed Samantha.

"Close enough," grumbled Fitzwallace. "Well go ahead; put the ring back on her finger and then kiss her breathless before she changes her mind."

Fitz hadn't even finished with his diatribe when King's mouth had descended on hers to seal the deal with a kiss.

"I remember the days you couldn't wait to get your hands on me," said JJ wistfully.

"Those days haven't passed, lass," Fitz said hauling her into his arms and kissing her with a passion that knew no bounds.

King didn't let Samantha come up for air, just kept kissing her between telling her how much he loved her and that he'd spank her ass silly if she ever put herself in danger again.

She didn't care. She was home; she was safe; she was in King's arms, and she would have her happily ever after.

EPILOGUE

*D*r. Bryan Mena took a deep breath. Too many years in the ER. Too many years pulling open a curtain and finding somebody he couldn't fix. Too many years fearing that somebody would be somebody he knew. Sliding back the curtain, he startled as he recognized the man lying with an almost casual air on the ER bed.

"Fuck, Royce, what are you doing here?"

"Bryan. Good. I was hoping it would be you."

"You're bleeding, Royce. What the hell happened?"

"What crawled up your ass, Bryan? You sound as if you aren't happy to see me."

Bryan watched as the young nurse wiped blood from the gnarly gnash on Royce's over-developed bicep. What was it with these guys? Did they do anything other than fuck and work out?

"What the hell happened this time?"

"A small dispute over one of the subs at Southside."

Bryan snorted.

"Since you asked, I won, and I doubt the asshole will think of trying to bother her again."

"In case you didn't notice, I didn't ask."

Bryan would never understand why so many of the guys from his former unit had opted to join the black ops group known around the world by one name: Cerberus. And most all of them played at or were resident Doms in either Baker Street in London, Club Southside here in Chicago, or both.

"You belong to Club Southside?" asked the nurse, just a bit too eagerly.

"I do. Have you ever been?" Royce asked in a deepened voice that seemed to ooze all around the nurse.

"She's my nurse, Royce, not one of your submissives."

"But I think she'd like to be, wouldn't you, sweetheart?" Royce asked seductively.

Bryan didn't know whether to be more outraged at the way Royce was speaking to her or the way the nurse seemed to almost tremble as her pupils dilated with arousal.

"It's awfully expensive, isn't it?"

This had gone too far. "That's enough, Royce. Knock it off and leave her alone."

Royce's attention on the nurse shifted from her to him and from seductive to angry.

"Watch yourself, Bryan. I know you don't approve of the lifestyle but if I hear that you've so much as said a word against this nice nurse who has done nothing wrong and ended up making things difficult for her, you'll wind up looking like the guy in the next bed. Keep in mind, I'm the one who put him there."

The next operative to find his better half is Royce. Click here to read The Scavenger.

She was in the wrong place at the wrong time. Now he must protect her but only if he can earn her trust!

When Royce is assigned to protect a new high-profile client, he doesn't understand how it's any different from any other case… until he meets the woman he's supposed to protect and hears her story.

Camille was in the wrong place at the wrong time. Two years ago she overheard a bratva kingpin order a hit on a senator's family. After the brutal killing by a Russian kill team she was taken into custody by the Feds and placed in WITSEC. Now she has been brought to Chicago to testify against the Russian mafia boss.

Royce is used to difficult clients, but Camille proves to be much more difficult than anyone he's ever met. She's a deadly combination of mouthwatering curves, wicked intelligence, and trusts no one.

What should be a straightforward assignment takes unscheduled turns when secrets, lies, and betrayal threaten to derail the job. If he is going to keep her safe, Royce has to convince Camille to trust him. He will need to use all of his skills and connections to keep the woman of his dreams alive but will trusting him bring another massacre, one that takes her life too?

BONUS SCENE

I have an **EXCLUSIVE** bonus scene as a thank you! All you have to do is click the link below, sign up for my newsletter, and you'll get an email giving you access!

SIGN UP HERE

Top Dog

Big Dog

Sea Dog

Ice Dog

Mystery, She Wrote

Invitation To Murder

Murder Before Dawn

Hook, Line and Mystery

Paint Me A Murder

Deadline To Murder

Relentless Pursuit (Duet)

To Love a Thief

My Fair Thief

Charade

Wild Mustang

Hampton

Mac

Croft

Noah

Thom

Reid

Crooked Creek Ranch

Taming His Cowgirl

Mystic River Shifters (small town shifter)

<u>Defiant Mate</u>

<u>Savage Mate</u>

<u>Reckless Mate</u>

<u>Shameless Mate</u>

<u>Runaway Mate</u>

<u>Stolen Mate</u>

<u>Bah Humbug Mate</u>

<u>Hidden Mate</u>

<u>Unforeseen Mate</u>

<u>Shadow Mate</u>

<u>Book Set Vol. 1</u>

<u>Book Set Vol. 2</u>

<u>Book Set Vol. 3</u>

Otter Cover Shifters (small town shifters/ spinoff Mystic River)

<u>Suspicious Mate</u>

<u>Unexpected Mate</u>

<u>Substitute Mate</u>

<u>Accidental Mate</u>

Feral Mate

Mystic Mate

Elusive Mate

Mysterious Mate

Syndicate Masters

Midwest

Kiss of Luck

Stroke of Fortune

Twist of Fate

Eastern Seaboard

High Stakes

High Roller

High Bet

La Cosa Nostra

Ruthless Honor

Feral Oath

Defiant Vow

Northern Lights

Alliance

Complication

Judgment

Syndicate Masters

The Bargain

The Pact

The Agreement

The Understanding

The Pledge

Box Set

Looking Glass Multiverse

Shifted Reality

Shifted Existence

Shifted Dimension

Box Set

Reign of Fire

Dragon Storm

Dragon Roar

Dragon Fury

Masters of Valor (spin off Masters of the Savoy)

Prophecy

Illusion

Deception

Inheritance

Masters of the Savoy

Advance

Negotiation

Submission

Contract

Bound

Release

Ghost Cat Canyon

Determined

Untamed

Bold

Fearless

Strong

Fated Legacy (spin-off Tangled Vines)

Touch of Fate

Touch of Darkness

Touch of Light

Touch of Fire

Touch of Ice

Touch of Destiny

Tangled Vines (spin-off Wayward Mates)

Corked

Uncorked

Decanted

Breathe

Full Bodied

Late Harvest

Mulled Wine

Wayward Mates

In Vino Veritas

Brought to Heel

ABOUT DELTA JAMES

Other books by Delta James: <u>https://www.</u>
<u>deltajames.com/</u>

As a USA Today bestselling romance author, Delta James aims to captivate readers with stories about complex heroines and the dominant alpha males who adore them. For Delta, romance is more than just a love story; it's a journey with challenges and thrills along the way.

After creating a second chapter for herself that was dramatically different than the first, Delta now resides in Florida where she relaxes on warm summer evenings with her loveable pack of basset hounds as they watch the birds, squirrels and lizards. When not crafting fast-paced tales, she enjoys horseback riding, walks on the beach, and white-water rafting.

Her readers mean the world to her, and Delta tries to interact personally to as many messages as she can. If you'd like to chat or discuss books, you can find Delta on Instagram, Facebook, and in her private reader group https://www.facebook.com/groups/348982795738444.

Keep up with Delta on Social Media

<u>Facebook page</u>

<u>Facebook group</u>

<u>Instagram</u>

<u>TikTok</u>

<u>Bookbub</u>

<u>Goodreads</u>

<u>Patreon</u>

<u>Signup</u> for my newsletter and

Get the good stuff…

Each month Delta shares her writing updates, novel releases, exclusive content and some fun personal stories.

Plus - there's often a giveaway!

Thank you!

ACKNOWLEDGMENTS

Thank you to my Patreon supporters.
I couldn't do this without you!

Carol Chase
Latoya McBride
Julia Rappaport
D F
Ellen
Margaret Bloodworth
Tamara Crooks
Rhonda
Autumn
Suzy Sawkins
Cindy Vernon
Linda Kniffen-Wager
Karen Somerville